KILLING FIELD

KILLING FIELD

Meghan Holloway

The following is a work of fiction. Names, characters, places, events and incidents are either the product of the author's imagination or used in an entirely fictitious manner. Any resemblance to actual persons, living or dead, is entirely coincidental.

Cover and jacket design by Mimi Bark

ISBN 978-1-951709-86-0
ISBN 978-1-957957-17-3
Library of Congress Control Number:
Available upon request

First trade paperback edition July 2022
by Polis Books, LLC
62 Ottowa Road S
Marlboro, NJ 07746

POLIS BOOKS

To Joe,
for trusting me as a storyteller and for championing
Hector's growth and journey throughout the series

And to JJ, for being my Frank

Prologue

WINONA

fifteen years ago

I guided my limping car to the shoulder and contemplated all the ways I would like to murder my husband.

The problem with love was not that it was blind. I saw Hector all too clearly. The problem with love was that it encouraged a woman to overlook a man's faults and love him in spite of them.

My car groaned, gave one last cough, and died. I dropped my forehead to the steering wheel and let out a ragged sigh. The affection I had once felt for Hector had withered throughout our years together. But my heart still ached for him, because every time I looked at him, I could see that void in him.

In my twenties, I thought sex would fill that void and make him love me. After fifteen years of marriage, I knew better. Nothing could fill the emptiness when life forged a hollow man. He had given me enough glimpses into his past for me to understand that my love would never be enough. Now it was all I could do to keep our daughter and myself from losing our way in that same desolate landscape.

I sniffed back senseless tears and rested a hand on my stomach. Hormones were making me more emotional than usual. I was still trying to figure out how to tell Hector the news. I had hoped fatherhood would plant the seeds for him.

A soil is only barren because it has not been tended, my mother used to tell me. She no longer whispered those words to me in Lakota when she caught a glimpse of the sadness I worked hard to hide. She hadn't done so for years now. She knew as well as I did that sometimes the land was simply fallow. No amount of tending could make a wasteland flourish.

Emma's nonsensical burst of chatter in the backseat broke the silence, startling me. There was no sense in moping. I had to get to the bakery before they closed and pick up the birthday cake for Emma's party. Hector had not bothered to remember to do so.

I pushed open my door, and the wind ripped it from my hands, flinging it open so forcefully the car rocked. The state road was deserted. I hurried to unbuckle Emma from her car seat.

"Mama!" she squealed, and buried her fists in my hair.

"*Cante skuye*!" I said, and tucked my face into her neck and blew a raspberry on her skin.

She shrieked with laughter, and I clutched her to me, breathing in her scent.

Emma should grow up knowing her mother. Fear and fury were a drumbeat pounding in my chest when I found the neatly typed note left in her car seat in the grocery store parking lot. I had saved all of the notes, each threat seared into my mind.

The wind whispered in my ears, and its song held an ominous tone.

I walked swiftly toward town. Emma began to whimper, picking up on my unease. She pushed against the tight grip I kept around her. I forced myself to loosen my hold and bounced her on my hip. She wanted to walk, though, and she was as stubborn as her father. Her face was soon red with anger.

I sang to distract her, making up a story about a little Lakota girl with black hair and green eyes who ran with the wolves and danced on the wind. After a few minutes, she was repeating the words to the song in her bird-like voice and clapping her pudgy hands.

I heard the approach of a vehicle behind us. The fear had become a constant companion. It no longer surprised me when it gripped me by the throat and squeezed my heart. I moved off the road, but the rolling plains of ranch land offered no place to hide. My arms tightened around Emma, and this time, I ignored her protests.

I had learned a lot about love as the wife of a man who was incapable of giving or receiving it. I thought I knew everything there was to know about love. Until I felt the first stirrings of a new life deep within me. This love was different. This love for my child, the one I held in my arms and the one that was barely a presence in my womb, was ferocious. It was armed with tooth and claw.

The fight went out of me, though, when I recognized

the vehicle that came around the bend. I sagged in relief and hurried back to the shoulder. The car slowed to a halt as soon as it reached me, and the passenger window buzzed down.

I smiled as I bent to meet the gaze of the driver. "I cannot tell you how glad I am to see you."

Part I

One

HECTOR

It was hot, the wind was high, and Yellowstone was ablaze.

I propped the portable radio on the windowsill and adjusted the rabbit-ear antennas until I was able to pick up the station relaying updates. A lightning strike in Lamar Valley two weeks ago had spread from a small forest fire to a thousand-acre inferno. A campfire left unattended along the Snake River south of the park had made its way across the national park's boundaries. Fires now burned near Old Faithful and along Yellowstone Lake.

The flames were miles from Raven's Gap, but tensions were already high. The town was situated along the northern perimeter of the park fifteen miles east of Gardiner, Montana. No one who had been here in 1988 had forgotten the horror of the fires that year.

For now, the Park Service was sticking to their wait and see policy, but the smell of smoke was thick in the air, and the sky was the color of an old bruise.

Frank whined at my side, and I rested a hand on the

standard poodle's head.

"All's well," I assured him.

The smell of smoke made him anxious now. Three months ago, a coordinated attack by Senator Grant Larson's men had left both Frank and me with bullet wounds and the Airstream trailer I called home burned to rubble. Now I had a scar on my arm, Frank had one across the back of his neck, and Larson was sitting in jail awaiting trial for murder.

"Do you think we'll have to evacuate?"

I turned at the sound of Evelyn Hutto's voice as she joined me in the kitchen.

For the last few months, Evelyn and I had shared The River Inn as our home after the previous innkeeper fled town. Faye Anders had left me the property. Since I had been homeless at the time, I moved into the wing of the inn Faye and her boy had lived in. I put a rug down over the stain on the bedroom floor, bought a new mattress and sheets, and tried to figure out what I was supposed to do with an inn.

Evelyn lived in a room on the opposite side of the inn and, along with two women she had hired, had taken up the bulk of responsibilities of dealing with guests. We shared the kitchen and little small talk, as both of us were more inclined toward silence.

"Not yet," I said in answer to her question about evacuating. "It depends on the wind."

She moved to the coffee pot and poured a mug. She leaned against the counter across from me, tilting her head as she listened to the update on the radio. With her hands wrapped around the coffee mug, I could not miss the spaces in her grip.

"I'm still surprised they don't put the fires out," she said.

"Not their policy," I said. "Fire is part of the ecosystem in Yellowstone."

She shuddered and ducked her head to peer at the sky through the window. "How do they—?"

My phone rang, and the contact number for Grover Westland, the county coroner, showed up on the screen.

"Sorry," I said.

She shook her head and left the kitchen.

"You know I'm not on the force any longer," I said by way of greeting as I answered the phone.

"Hector," he said. The tone of his voice made me straighten. "Can you come in?"

"What have you found?" I asked. My hand was clenched around the handle of the coffee mug. I forced myself to set the mug aside before I snapped the handle.

"I don't want to do this over the phone," he said quietly.

"I'll be there as soon as I can."

Frank hated the smell of the morgue on me, but he hated being left alone now that the rank odor of smoke filled the air.

"Come on, boy," I said as I grabbed my wallet and keys.

He stuck close to my side as we left the inn until he spotted the girl standing on the front walk. His ears pricked, and his tail started wagging. I paid her no mind as I crossed to my truck.

"Excuse me," she called.

"You'll have to talk to the woman inside about vacancies," I said, motioning for Frank to load up. I climbed in after him and slammed the door.

As I pulled out of the inn's drive and headed down the street, I glanced in the rearview mirror. The girl stood on the sidewalk staring after me.

It took me an hour to reach the main sheriff's department in Livingston. Once inside the building, I left Frank with one of the women at the front desk and headed to the basement. I knew why Frank hated the smell. It was one I could never acclimate to either, and I breathed shallowly through my mouth when I entered the morgue.

Grover looked up from his desk. He stood quickly and extended his hand. "Thanks for coming in."

I shook his hand, uncomfortable with the formality we had never shared before. "What did you find?"

He sighed. "Do you want to sit?"

"No," I said, and impatience crept into my voice. "Just tell me what the fuck you found. Emma? Winona?"

At first, everyone had speculated that Winona had grown tired of me and finally moved on to find someone who was more deserving of her. But my wife was not one for elaborate gestures or manipulation. She was blunt and straightforward. She would have told me she was leaving me. She loved her hometown, and she would never have put her friends or family through the agony of thinking something had happened to her. She would have packed her bags, made no secret of the fact, and gone to Maggie's to sleep on her couch.

I had known something was terribly wrong from

the beginning. By the second day she and Emma were missing, so had everyone else.

Fifteen years had passed. There had been a drudgery of suspicion, bitterness, and tireless searching. I knew the statistics. Hope was a luxury for the naïve and ill-informed.

Grover put a hand on my shoulder. I fought the urge to shake it off. "A month ago, a woman in Contact called the department. Her Labrador found remains in the woods."

For years, I had known that when I finally managed to bring Emma and Winona home, it would be in a box. But it was still a blow.

"Sit down, man," he said, and this time I obeyed.

"Emma or Winona?"

He kept his hand on my shoulder. "Winona."

My eyes slid closed. When Winona and I were married, I repeated the words of the officiant without giving them any thought. The vows meant nothing to me. They were empty words. All I had been thinking about as I said them was getting Winona out of the dress she wore. It was the first time I had seen her in a dress. It was yellow, molded to her breasts, cinching in the deep curve of her waist, flaring out over her hips. The hem flirted around her knees and was edged in lace. All I could think about as I repeated the words was how easy it would be to flip the skirt of her dress up and have her. When she met my gaze and grinned, I knew she could tell exactly what I was thinking.

To have and to hold, from this day forward, for better, for worse, for richer, for poorer, in sickness and in health, to love and to cherish, till death do us part.

I had been poor and worse. I was young, so I thought myself invincible to sickness, imagined I would always be in good health, and had no inkling that a few years later my luck would run out in the dirt beneath the hooves and horns of a raging bull. I did not know anything about love, nor did I know how to cherish someone. I had little in the world I could claim as my own, and I intended to hold on to what I did have.

For fifteen years, the notion of *till death do us part* had made me bitter. I had no clue when I said those words that death parting us would have been easy. I had no notion that there were more gut-wrenching things than death that could separate a man and woman.

In the end, I had not been certain I wanted Winona and Emma as my own any longer. I was not built to be a husband, and I had been apathetic about fatherhood. Now, it seemed ludicrous that my girls had once felt like a ball and chain around my neck. I would have given anything to have a second chance, but all I could do was hope they had not suffered.

In the first days and weeks, I had been terrified I would find them dead. But in the months and years that followed, I had been desperate. Dread at finding my girls had turned to despair at not finding them. They lingered still, not alive but not dead, not gone but not in my arms where I should have cherished and protected them and failed to do so. They were ghosts who dogged my step, caught in this unknown purgatory with no fucking answers.

So I had made another vow. This one was an oath I intended to keep all the way to my own grave. I would not rest, and I would not give up. I would do whatever it took to find out what happened to my girls and bring them home.

"Let me see," I said.

He patted my shoulder and then moved to the mortuary cabinet and pulled open one of the drawers. "I had the forensics team run the tests three times just to be certain, and I verified the results myself." He drew the sheet aside, and the material whispered ominously.

I could not drag my eyes away. "I need a moment," I said. My voice was hoarse.

"Take all the time you need," he said.

When I was alone in the room with what remained of my wife, I stood and approached. The skull looked incredibly fragile on the metal table. The lower jaw was missing, but the bone that remained was bleached clean by exposure. My fingers trembled as I reached out and lifted the skull.

I had to sit down. I leaned my elbows on my knees and cradled my wife's head in my hands, struggling to remember the silken glide of her hair through my fingers. I stroked my palm over the globe of her skull. I tried to ignore the scrape of tooth marks I could see in places where an animal had gnawed her flesh from the bone. A gouge marred the back of her skull. A deep dent had caved in her left temple with fractures radiating out from the wound. There were places where the bone fragments were missing, but Grover had restructured what he could. The blow to the back of her head would have stunned her, knocked her unconscious. The blow to her temple was a killing one.

My fingers trembled as I stroked my thumbs along

the ridge of her cheekbones. My wife's American Indian heritage had been evident in the structure of her facial features, her skin tone, and the lustrous fall of dark hair around her shoulders. Everything that had been her was stripped away now. The slight smile always on her lips that so easily spread into a quicksilver grin. Her eyes, so dark a brown they were almost black, lighting up like a beacon when she smiled. The laugh lines etched deeply into the skin around her eyes.

I traced a finger along the curve of her eye sockets before lifting her skull and pressing my nose against her fractured temple. I inhaled deeply and tried to remember the warmth and softness of her skin, the texture of her hair against my face, the scent of cinnamon that always clung to her hair.

But there was nothing.

Frank seemed to sense my mood as I drove home. He sprawled across the seat with his paw on my knee and his chin resting on the box at my side.

When we first started training for the search and rescue team, I tried HRD—human remains detection—training with Frank, but the poodle had a strong aversion to decomposing tissue. He did not care to be around the dead, and I could not much blame him. He had merely sniffed the box containing Winona's skull, though, and then settled down beside me.

I had never been a man to drown myself in alcohol. My first memory was of cleaning up my mother's vomit when she had returned from a bender. I had been four at the time. The last memory I had of her was from ten years later with her face gray and her blue lips speckled with her own vomit.

As I drove into Raven's Gap and passed Thornton's Market, though, I quickly pulled into the parking lot. The liquor store next door beckoned to me.

Frank sat up as I parked the truck. I hesitated and rested a hand on the box. "Keep an eye on her for me," I told him.

"Hey!" a voice called as I crossed the parking lot. "Hey, mister!"

I glanced back and recognized the girl I had seen in front of the inn this morning. "Not interested."

"Please, just listen," she said, hurrying toward me. "I need—"

"I don't want any Girl Scout cookies," I said. "Or anything else you're selling. Hit someone else up to meet your quota."

"No, that's—"

I entered the liquor store and the slam of the door behind me cut off the rest of her words. As I headed down the aisle, I could not help looking through the window. The girl had crossed her arms over her chest, and her shoulders were slumped. I turned my gaze to the selection of whiskey on the shelves.

I grabbed a bottle of Johnnie Walker and paid at the register. When I exited the liquor store, the girl was nowhere to be seen. I headed toward my truck.

"You're Hector, right? Hector Lewis?"

I sighed and turned. She was young, a Native American in her late teens at the oldest, with a long sheet of dark hair pulled to the side in a frayed braid.

"What do you want?" I asked.

She stopped a short distance from me. "You're Hector Lewis?"

"Last time I checked."

"I need your help."

I studied her. Her smile was uncertain around the edges. Her arms and legs were bird-thin, and her clothes looked as if they had been handed down half a dozen times before they reached her.

"I'm not social services, kid."

Her eyes narrowed. She took a step closer to me, clutching a backpack like a shield at her chest. "I don't need social services."

I turned and continued across the parking lot to my truck. "Then the police department is three blocks that way." I nodded in the direction of Main Street.

Frank's head was still resting on the box when I opened the door. He looked past me and stood up, tail wagging.

"No, I don't—I'm Emma."

I froze, the name like a knife slid between my ribs. I pivoted until I faced her again.

"I'm your daughter," she whispered.

Two

HECTOR

"I'm your daughter." She whispered the words a second time, and they almost cut my knees out from under me.

I held on to the doorframe and stared at her until Frank nudged my shoulder. I had to tear my gaze away, and I rubbed my hand over my jaw to compose myself.

"You hungry?" My voice was rough. "I was about to go to the diner."

The girl hesitated, but I could see the temptation on her thin face. "That's it? That's all you're going to say?"

"My stomach is going to start gnawing on my backbone soon," I said. "Yes or no?"

She shrugged in a stiff attempt at nonchalance. "I could eat."

The careful casualness of the words made me wonder how long it had been since she had eaten.

"Come on, then. Frank, get in the backseat."

She hurried around the front of my truck and opened the passenger door, but she hesitated with one foot on the running board. "You're not a freak, are you?"

I cranked the truck. "Shouldn't you have thought about that before you approached me?"

Her chin jutted out and she heaved herself up into the passenger's seat, slamming the door behind her with a thump of bravado. She buckled her seatbelt but sat as close to the door as she could get and still be inside the vehicle. I pulled out onto the state road and could see she watched me from the corner of her eye.

"What's in this?" she asked suddenly, and reached toward the box occupying the bench between us.

I slapped a hand on the lid. "Don't touch it," I snapped with more bite in my voice than I intended.

She shrank against the door and folded her arms tightly around herself. "Jesus. Sorry."

I rolled my shoulders, trying to force the tension that was gripping my neck to loosen and wishing I'd already cracked open the bottle of Johnnie now resting in the backseat.

Frank stuck his big head between the headrest and the side of the truck and sniffed the girl's ear.

She lurched forward, shoulders hunched. "Does that dog bite?"

"His name is Frank. And not usually."

I pulled into the diner's front lot, and she was out of the vehicle before I could put the truck in park.

I rubbed the lid of the box. I had asked Grover not to make any more calls and to wait on releasing the results to the newspapers. I needed to be the one to break the news to Winona's friends and family. I just did not know how I was going to tell them.

Grover told me a special team had been brought in to search the area where the Labrador had found

Winona's skull. A month of combing the northern edge of the Custer Gallatin National Forest and the Boulder River had turned up nothing.

I traced the edges of the box. She had been left out in the elements for so long, exposed to the sun and moon, wind and rain, snow and fire. I wondered if she had been alive for any of it, if she had lain wounded in the dark. If she had listened to a wolf's lonesome call, knowing her time was approaching, and not realizing that her husband, a man she loved but who had never loved her back, would search for her. I wondered if she thought I would be relieved that she was gone. The notion crushed me, and my eyes burned.

A rap on my window startled me.

"You said you were starving," the girl called through the glass. "You coming or what?"

I glanced back at Frank, who smiled at me. "Sit tight," I told him. "I'll bring you your usual." I left the engine running with the air conditioner on high for him.

I tucked the box under my arm and exited the truck. The girl followed me across the parking lot, jogging to keep up with my longer stride.

Maggie Silva greeted us when we entered. Three months ago, when I discovered how Senator Grant Larson threatened my wife after she uncovered his poaching operation, my anger had erupted. I drove to the man's front door, broke his jaw, and then had almost been beaten to death. Had my brother-in-law not saved me, I likely would be the dead bait left out to draw in the trophy of Larson's next hunt.

Maggie had been by my side when I first woke up

in the hospital, surprised to realize I was still alive. She had been Winona's closest friend and the one person who had never doubted my innocence. She was steadfast and loyal, and she was still angry with me for, in her words, being such an idiot.

Her gaze was bright with curiosity as she glanced back and forth between us. "You brought a guest today."

"I'm his daughter," the girl said.

Maggie's brows went up, and her smile fell straight off her face. Her gaze flew to mine, eyes wide.

"Go get us a booth, kid," I said. "I need to wash my hands."

Once she was out of earshot, Maggie whispered, "Hector, what the hell?"

I sighed. "Keep an eye on her. If she tries to sneak out, grab her. I need to use your phone."

I bypassed the kitchen and the restrooms and headed into Maggie's office. I knew my father-in-law would not answer the phone if he recognized my number, so I grabbed the receiver from the phone on the desk and dialed.

When he answered, I said, "It's me. Don't hang up."

"What do you want?" Ed Decker asked, voice cold and hard.

"I'm giving you a head's up. There's a girl who just showed up in town. She's in some kind of trouble." I hung my head and rubbed the back of my neck. "She says she's Emma." He sucked in a breath, but I continued before he could get a word in. "I wanted you to hear it from me, not be blindsided."

I needed to say it. I needed to tell him the news that

would both devastate him and finally bring him relief. Wasn't that what I felt? The double-edge blade of pain at the confirmation that she was gone and solace at having a piece of her back with me.

I was not a religious man. I did not believe in an afterlife or a lingering of a spirit. Death was just that, the end of a life. I did not think anything that had made Winona the woman I knew her to be was contained in the box I held. No personality or essence remained. Even so, I found myself reluctant to share what was left of her with others, though they deserved to know.

I took a deep breath. "Ed," I began, but then the dial tone began to drone in my ear. He had already ended the call.

Three

ANNIE

Sixty years old was practically ancient, but Hector Lewis was nothing like the grandfatherly figure I had been expecting.

I had never known my grandfather, but I liked to think he would have been caring, that his hugs would have been tight enough to feel like they kept the world at bay, and that he would have had a laugh that could be heard half a mile away.

I wasn't certain Hector even knew how to smile, let alone laugh. He was also an asshole. I had never intended to actually claim I was his daughter. His repeated dismissal of me without even giving me time to tell him why I wanted to talk with him had made me desperate.

Once the words left my mouth, there was no calling them back. I simply wanted him to listen to me, and now there was no way to say, "Sorry, my name is actually Annie Between Lodges. I'm not your daughter, but I still need your help."

My stupidity made my throat tight. It was hard to

swallow as I ate. I tried to eat in measured bites, but I had barely scraped together the cash for the bus ticket. The old woman with muffins and sweet rolls in her bag had stayed on the Greyhound when I got off in Cheyenne. That was five days ago.

Since then, I had gulped water from the sink faucets of gas station bathrooms and tried to ignore the gnawing, hollow protests of my stomach. I would have grabbed a pack of crackers to relieve my hunger, but there were cameras everywhere now. I couldn't afford to be picked up for shoplifting.

When I looked up from my plate, I found Hector watching me. I forced myself to smile widely and brightly at him. He didn't return the gesture. His only response was a slight arch of his eyebrows.

I didn't need him to smile, I reminded myself. I needed him to be unafraid and untouchable.

He had a hard face. It was lined and weathered. The goatee that should have softened his face a little didn't.

He cleared his throat, and with a start, I realized I was still staring at him and the smile had slipped off my face. Before I could say anything, he slid his untouched plate across the table. Embarrassment made my face hot, but he held up his hand when I started to protest.

"You're hungry enough, eat it," he said. He had a voice that sounded like it scraped his throat on the way out.

I wondered what he had been called. Papa? Dad? How was I going to get out of this? "Thanks...*Até*."

He knew the Lakota word for *father*. I could tell immediately. His face tightened, and a muscle in his jaw ticked as he turned and glanced across the room, catching the black woman's eye.

It seemed like she ran the place, and there was something between her and Hector. She nodded when she met his gaze, and then her eyes darted to me and narrowed.

I looked down at my plate and shoved a fry in my mouth. I would have to be careful of her. She had a nice face but the eyes of a hawk.

I had always liked hawks. They were messengers. The trouble with hawks, though, was that they were extremely curious.

The bell over the door chimed, and an even quieter hush fell over the diner. Before I could turn to see who had arrived, Hector leaned toward me. I fought the urge to shrink back.

"Listen to me," he said quietly, and the hair rose on the back of my neck at his tone. "We have our differences, but I won't see them hurt."

I turned and saw an older couple approaching. *Old* old, not Hector old.

The man was small and wiry, and he wore a trapper hat complete with earflaps, even though it was the middle of summer. He was white, but the woman beside him was not. She was slightly taller than the old man. Her face sad and lined and gaunt. Illness clung to her, and a brightly colored scarf was wrapped around her head.

Oh no, no, no. "Are they—?"

"Winona's parents," Hector said. His voice was flat. "Betty and Ed."

Winona. Emma Lewis's mother. I remembered her face from the news clip and the research I had done.

My first thought when I saw her photo on the screen was how kind her eyes were. How she looked like she smiled a lot.

I was an idiot. I shouldn't have come here.

I swallowed and stood, suddenly wishing I hadn't scarfed down that turkey club already. It sat heavily in my stomach now, and I was afraid it might make a reappearance.

The old man and woman stopped as soon as I stood. My knees shook a little as I approached them.

I wasn't certain what to say. This was different from Hector. These people were old, and there was so much hope and pain in their eyes it hurt me to look at them. I should admit it now. I should just blurt it out. *I'm sorry, I lied. I'm not Emma.*

The old man approached me, but the woman stopped him with a hand on his arm. He glanced at her, and something unspoken passed between them.

She moved toward me, back straight, head high. She didn't look like a Betty. She looked like a Ptesáŋwiŋ. She looked exactly like how I envisioned the White Buffalo Calf Woman would look. Wise and timeless and striking in a way that was strong and fierce.

She was a couple of inches taller than me, and when she cupped my face in her hands, I had to look up into her eyes.

I opened my mouth to tell her, to admit that I was not her beloved Emma.

"*Mit'ákoja*," she whispered. Her gaze slipped past me and landed behind me, lingering for a moment, before returning to my face. "You are a beautiful young woman."

The tears that filled my eyes surprised me, and her thumb brushed the one away that spilled from the corner of my eye. I couldn't remember the last time someone had touched me so gently.

"*Uncí*," I said. The word slipped out of me before I could stop it, and my voice broke a little to call this woman grandmother.

She pulled me into her arms. Even whittled by illness, her arms were strong and secure around me. I rested my head on her shoulder. This, I realized. *This* was what I had longed for over the last five years.

The last weeks and months—maybe even the years—caught up with me, and the fabric beneath my cheek grew damp.

I felt split open like a carcass lying too long in the heat of the sun. Everything raw and bleeding inside me suddenly felt as if it were exposed.

There was a touch on the back of my head. I looked up, and the old man's face swam waveringly in my vision.

"You used to call me Papa," he said.

I reached out and wrapped an arm around his narrow shoulders. He enfolded both his wife and me in his arms.

For a moment, I imagined the arms around me were my grandmother's and my mother's. But they were gone now and so was my sister.

I struggled to control my tears. If I cracked now, I was afraid it would be like a dam bursting. I would never be able to contain the emotion once it slipped free.

I could feel Hector's hard gaze on my back, but I

didn't turn and look at him. Instead, I closed my eyes and memorized the sensation of this tight hug that was so full of longing and hope.

I already felt guilty, but I had not been prepared to wish I truly were Emma Lewis.

Four

HECTOR

"What are you doing?" I asked, keeping my voice low, when Ed moved to stand beside me.

"What do you think?" he countered. "Reuniting with our granddaughter."

Betty tucked her arm around the girl's waist. "I need some cold water on my face. We'll be back in a moment," she said, and led the girl toward the bathrooms.

Once she and the girl were out of earshot, Ed slid into the booth. I took a seat opposite him. Maggie crossed to our table and placed a mug before Ed.

He glanced up at her as she filled it with coffee. "I think I'm going to need something a little stronger than that, my dear."

She reached into her apron and drew a bottle of whiskey from the pocket. "That's why I got this from my desk." She added a liberal splash to his mug and to mine and then hurried to another table.

I drained my mug, and Ed did the same.

"This isn't good for Betty," I told him.

He glanced over his shoulder, but the pair were still

in the bathroom. "Betty decides what is good for Betty."

I acknowledged that with a nod. Her daughter had been much the same.

"She's just a child, Hector," he said.

"She's lying."

"Yes," he agreed. "But she must have a reason for it. Until she decides to tell us what that reason is, I'll treat her the same way I would if she were Emma, finally coming home to us."

I was cast adrift. *I'm your daughter. I'm Emma.* I knew the statistics. After the first five years, I had never allowed myself to hope to hear those words. Emma was never coming home. Neither was Winona. My girls were gone, and the only thing I had to hold on to was the determination to find out who had taken them from me.

Bitterness was a constant ache in my gut, and now I felt it simmering into anger. This punk ass kid had no clue the agonizing blow she had dealt. I had seen the hope on Ed's and Betty's faces when they walked into the diner. The despair they had quickly masked when they, too, had confirmed the girl was not Emma.

When she returned to the table, I fully intended to rip the kid a new one. But then movement across the diner caught my eye, and I watched as Betty and the girl made their way toward us.

In the parking lot of the grocery store, I thought the girl had looked hard and brittle, old beyond her years and wary in a way that told me she was on the run.

Looking at her now, watching the way she held one of Betty's hands in both of hers and leaned into her as they crossed the diner, I thought she looked like a lost, desperate child. The stony facade was gone, and her face was wide open, yearning and tender.

"Shit," I breathed. I wished I had not drained my mug of its mixture of whiskey and coffee.

"Have a care with her," Ed said softly. When I glanced at him, I saw him watching the pair moving toward us as well. "She's not our Emma, but she's someone's little girl."

She still wore her backpack. She had not taken it off when she sat down, and she did not take it off now when she slid into the booth beside me. I slid over and kept the box on the bench between us. The girl kept a hand wrapped around Betty's as the older woman sat across from her.

My mother-in-law was a proud, quiet woman. She had never spoken to me much, even in the days, months, and years after Winona and Emma went missing. She turned to me now.

"Emma is going to stay with us," she said.

When Ed did not react, I knew they had discussed it on the way over. I tried not to let my relief show. I didn't know what to do with a kid.

The girl who claimed she was Emma beamed. "Really?" She looked at me. "Do you mind, *Até*?"

Fifteen years was a long time. I kept a photo of my girls on the table beside my bed, the same picture that was used for the missing persons banners that had gone up on billboards across the state, across the country. It had been one of the first things I grabbed when my Airstream was set ablaze. When I moved into the inn, Maggie had given me a frame for the photograph. I traced the lines of their faces every day to keep them firmly etched in my mind.

I remembered the dimple in Winona's left cheek, the swing of her hips as she walked, the stretch of her body as she sat on the edge of the bed every night and brushed her hair to gleaming. I remembered my daughter's fondness for huckleberries, how she loved to sit on her grandfather's knee as he played the banjo, how her shadow had made her laugh and laugh.

I could remember all of that. I could remember my coldness toward them and the twin deflated expressions on their faces before I turned away.

But I could not remember the sound of their voices, the lilt of Emma's squeals and giggles, the cadence of Winona's singing and laughter. I could not remember what Emma's voice had sounded like when she said *Até*.

Winona had asked me if I preferred the English equivalent, but my wife's heritage was something that influenced everything she did. It was simply part of who she was, and I had no qualms with her raising our daughter to have that same connection to her roots.

Até was Emma's first word. I knew her voice had been sweet and small, pure and birdlike. But I could not remember the way it sounded.

I stared at the girl before me now. I wanted to tell her to never call me that again. It was not her name to call me.

I took a breath, ready to tell her the charade was up, but once again I found myself caught by the expression on her face. Her eyes were red-rimmed from crying. Now I could clearly see the dark circles under her eyes, the sunken hollows of her cheeks, the sallowness beneath her burnished skin. Her lips were chapped, and as I studied her face, that practiced smile slipped.

When I let myself really look at her, I saw a scared little girl.

"No." I swallowed. I could not force the name past my lips, though. "No, kid, I don't mind."

—

I could have waited on the porch of his cabin, but I jimmied the lock on his front door and took a seat in his recliner. Frank sprawled on the floor at my feet, and I drank straight from the bottle of Johnnie Walker. It was not long before I heard his truck in the drive and his tread across the front porch.

Jack Decker sighed when he opened the door. "I thought we were past this now."

He had adored his older sister, and when Winona introduced me to the family, he had been just a teenager. He had hated me on sight.

Since Winona and Emma had disappeared, his hatred had festered into something entirely more dangerous. I recognized obsession. I understood it. I had known this man would try to kill me one day. He had simply bided his time until he thought he could do it and get away with it.

But three months ago, the opportunity had been handed to him, and he had not taken it. Instead, he saved my life, and in doing so, helped me bring down his boss's multi-million-dollar poaching operation. We had reached an uneasy truce since then.

"It's a special occasion," I said quietly, rolling the whiskey bottle between my palms. I looked up at him.

For the last few hours, I had tried to think of what to say. In the end, I simply told him the truth. "The coroner called me today." He flinched as if I had struck him. When he remained quiet, I continued, "Remains were found near Contact about a month ago. They were thorough with the testing. I saw the results myself. It's Winona."

His jaw was clenched, his hands fisted. "Was she…?" He swallowed and started again. "How did she die?"

"She was struck in the head." Since they had not been able to find the rest of her body, the coroner could not say with certainty what the cause of death was. I pointed the bottle of whiskey toward the box sitting on his kitchen counter. "That's all they've been able to find."

He crossed slowly to the box and stood staring at it for a long moment. A muscle ticked in his cheek, and though he placed a hand on the lid, he did not open the box. When he glanced at me, the uncertainty in his face made me think of a young boy.

"You don't need to look," I told him. "It's just bone, not her."

His throat worked, and he rubbed his hand over the lid of the box. After several silent minutes, he walked out the front door. Frank stood and whined, but I placed a hand on his head when he would have followed Jack.

"He needs a moment alone," I said.

The poodle settled at my feet once more. It was half an hour before Jack returned. He carried the rocker from the front porch in with him, and when he took a seat, he extended his hand toward me. I passed him the bottle of Johnnie without a word.

We sat in silence, passing the bottle of whiskey between us.

"Emma?" Jack finally asked, voice rough. "Did they find her yet?"

Até. The girl's voice resonated through my mind, and for an instant, I wished she actually were my daughter. For a brief moment, there in the liquor store parking lot when she had made that earth-shattering announcement, I had felt something akin to hope flair in my chest. It had been quickly snuffed out as soon as I caught a closer glimpse of the girl's face. Her eyes were not the green Emma's had been, and the scar through her eyebrow from where Emma had fallen into the corner of the cabinets when she was first learning how to walk was absent.

"There's something else I need to tell you," I said.

Five

ANNIE

"This will be your room," Ed said, pushing open a door at the end of the hallway. "The bathroom here is all yours. Anything you need, you let us know."

I nodded, unable to speak. He rested a hand on my shoulder and then retreated. I stood in the doorway for a long moment, backpack clutched to my chest.

The house was overwhelming. It was cool inside, and the whisper of the air conditioner over my skin raised the hair on my arms. The walls were so sturdy I could not hear any bird song from outside, although the faint smell of wildfire smoke had crept into the house. The floor did not tilt and sag beneath my feet. The bed was a proper one, not a pile of blankets on the floor or a threadbare mattress I had dragged from the dump with its coils poking out.

The room was brightly lit by lamplight. I could tell both the rug on the floor and the quilt on the bed were handmade. The furniture was sparse, but the room was clean. A floppy-eared stuffed bunny was propped against the pillows.

The entire place both enthralled me and made me uneasy. It was so normal, and so foreign.

I crossed the room slowly and uncertainly and picked up the stuffed animal. He had been patched many times over, seams stitched and holes repaired with patterned fabric. The bunny was clearly well-loved. I fingered the velvety ears and wondered at the little girl who had loved this stuffed animal with such ferocity and at the people who obviously had loved that little girl.

"We found Chapa in the backseat floorboard of the car Winona was driving the day they disappeared."

I jumped at the sound of Betty's voice and hurriedly placed the stuffed animal back on the bed. "I'm sorry."

"No need to be," she said. "I didn't mean to startle you. I made you a cup of tea."

I shifted the backpack from my chest to my shoulders once again before accepting the steaming mug from her. I stepped aside as she picked up the stuffed animal.

"Chapa?" I asked. I took a sip of the hot tea, and warmth filled me in the wake of the sweetly bitter liquid. "I thought it was a rabbit, not a beaver."

Betty stroked the long, floppy ears. "It is a rabbit." She carefully propped the stuffed animal against the pillows. She turned to me. "Ed and I are so glad to have you here. We hope you'll be comfortable."

I swallowed and glanced around. As uncertain as this house made me feel, another part of me wished I could live in a place so grand and clean and secure. "I will," I whispered.

She closed the door behind her as she left the room.

I sagged, sitting down heavily on the bed. My shoulders slumped. The weight of my backpack dug the straps into my skin. I hung my head, rolling my neck to try to relieve the ache I felt from head to toe.

The bathroom was as clean as the bedroom, no ring of grime in the shower or rust stain in the sink. I locked the door behind me and stuffed my backpack behind a stack of towels under the sink. Habit had me leaving the curtain of the shower partially open so I could see if the doorknob started to wiggle.

The water ran clear with an easy turn of the taps. No hauling water from a well. No struggle to warm it. No hurried washing because the water was so cold it made my skin turn painfully numb at first contact.

The hot water eased the pain in my shoulders and neck, and the grime of the last weeks swirled down the drain in the wake of soap and shampoo. I sighed at the luxury.

I was reluctant to put my dirty clothes back on, but they were the only clothing I had with me. I grimaced as I dressed and retrieved my backpack.

A neat stack of clothes on the end of the bed greeted me when I returned to my room. I picked up the t-shirt at the top of the pile. The tags were still attached. I rifled through the rest of the pile. The shirts, shorts, and leggings were all brand new. There was even a pack of underwear and socks and a new bra at the bottom of the pile.

Throat tight, I dragged the chair in the corner across the floor and wedged it against the door. I stripped off my dirty clothes and dressed in the brand new ones purchased just for me.

It wasn't that late, but I secreted my backpack away and crawled into the neatly made bed fully clothed. I leaned over and turned the lamp off, flooding the room in darkness. I couldn't help turning the switch on and off, marveling at the ease of having light with just a toggle until I realized I was being ridiculous. Embarrassed, I turned the light off for good this time. I stared at the seam of dim light around the door and reached out, groping in the darkness across the quilt until I felt the stuffed animal.

I clutched the bunny to my chest and buried my face in its velveteen fur while I waited for sleep.

The low murmur of voices woke me.

I was surprised the heat had not woken me. My little sister felt like a flame, she was so hot where her small body was pressed against my back. I sat up. My nightgown was damp with sweat.

In the dark, I couldn't make Kimi out. She was just a lump beside me on the mattress. I reached out and touched her, frightened by how hot she was. Her breath wheezed and rattled out of her.

"Mama?"

I didn't hear the hum of the generator, and our house stayed dark. My mother was a shadow in the doorway.

"What's wrong with Kimi?" I whispered.

"She's going to be fine," my mother said quietly. She leaned over the bed and rested her hand on Kimi's back. She pressed her lips to my forehead. "She's sick, but I'm going to get her some medicine. She's going to be fine."

She lifted Kimi from the bed. My little sister moaned fretfully.

I scrambled after my mother as she left the room. "I'll

go with you!"

My grandmother sat in the corner in her rocker. My mother placed Kimi in her arms. "I'll be back as quickly as I can," she said to my grandmother before she turned to me. She knelt in front of me and cupped my face in her hands. I felt her fingers tremble. "I need you to stay here and look after your sister. Will you do that for me?"

I nodded. "I will. I promise. I'll take good care of her."

"I know you will."

She pressed her forehead to mine and then stood and hurried out the door.

I followed her to the doorway, tucking my feet over one another to keep the chill from biting my toes too hard. She disappeared all too quickly in the darkness.

A sound startled me from that hazy world between wakefulness and dreaming. I lifted my head from the pillow. "Mama?" I whispered.

I sat up, disoriented in the dark room, and it took me a moment before I realized where I was. I had watched the lane for my mother until morning. She had never returned home. Not that night, or any night since.

The sound came again. I slipped from the bed and felt carefully underneath, reassuring myself the backpack was still hidden. I moved the chair from in front of the door and cracked the door to peer into the hallway.

Light gleamed in the stairwell, and I could hear the low murmur of voices. I hesitated and then slipped from my room and crept down the stairs. I reached the bottom of the stairs and glanced around. The house was simply laid out with the stairs leading down into the living room at the front of the house. The voices and light were coming from the rear of the house in the kitchen.

I picked my way silently down the hall and paused in the shadows out of sight from the doorway. A man spoke, his voice unfamiliar, and I shifted until I could peer into the kitchen.

Ed and Betty sat at the kitchen table. A man sat with them, one hand gripping Ed's shoulder, the other holding Betty's hand. Ed's head bowed, and his shoulders began to shake. He was weeping, I realized, heart in my throat.

Betty pushed back from her chair and moved to her husband's side, wrapping her arms tightly around him. The light over the stove glinted on her damp cheeks.

Their grief was raw in their faces. I wondered if this was because of me, because I had made the mistake of claiming to be the granddaughter they had been missing for so long. I took a quick step back, swamped with shame and feeling guilty for intruding on this private moment.

The floorboard under my foot creaked. I froze, holding my breath, and my gaze flew back to the trio at the table.

Betty's head was bent over Ed's, and they gripped one another, rocking back and forth. They were lost in their heartbreak.

The man was staring straight at me, though. He saw me standing in the shadows, and his eyes narrowed when I met his gaze. He had to be Ed and Betty's son. He had the same features as Betty, only harder and sharper. He didn't move from his spot beside his parents.

I retreated into the shadows. When I was locked back in my borrowed room, lying in bed with the stuffed bunny clutched to my chest, it took me a long time to find sleep again.

Six

HECTOR

The white wolf was waiting for me across the river. I was not even surprised to see her. I had come to expect her presence.

She had appeared like a ghost in the darkness almost every night over the last five months. One evening when I was throwing a ball for Frank, she had loped out of the forest. I had automatically reached for my gun, leery as she approached my dog. They stood shoulder to shoulder for a moment, tails erect but no hackles raised or snarls. Frank broke the tension by dropping into a playful stance, and soon they were racing back and forth through the meadow.

I had never seen anything like it. She never approached me, and I knew better than to leave food out for her. But she kept returning, and I kept looking for her.

When Frank and I had moved into the inn, I thought that would be the last we saw of her. My property had been miles outside of town, remote and isolated. I knew a wolf's territory was distinct, and I could not imagine she would venture so close to town.

The first night we had slept in the inn, I had been restless in the unfamiliar surroundings. As I paced the floor of the great room, movement on the opposite shore of the river caught my eye. I slipped out onto the back deck. The inn was situated on an oxbow of the Yellowstone, and moonlight gleamed on the river and the pristine white fur of the wolf on the far bank.

My wife had been Lakota, but she had told me once of the Diné legend of skin-walkers, humans disguising themselves as an animal. My brother-in-law had told me of the *wakan* in Lakota culture, a man or a woman capable of mediating between the supernatural and the common people. They did not appear as wolves, but there was a group of the *wakan* who all experienced similar visions. Š*ung'manitu ihanblapi*. They dream of wolves.

All Native peoples revered the wolf. They admired them for their strength and endurance, for their courage and loyalty, and for their devotion to family.

I opened the french doors I had installed the other week. The wind was blowing the rank odor of smoke away from town tonight. Frank followed at my heels as I moved out onto the back deck.

The white wolf stood still and watchful, and even at this distance, I thought I could feel her keen predator gaze fixed on me unwaveringly. She was magnificent. Powerfully and leanly built, at the top of the food chain, but elegant and majestic to behold. Frank spotted her and let out a soft bark of greeting. The white wolf's head tilted as she watched us.

I rested the box containing Winona's skull on the

railing. What haunted me was that I had never been able to return her love. Whatever she had endured, she had not known with absolute certainty that I would never stop fighting to find her and our daughter.

"Hector?"

Frank leapt up at the sound of Maggie's voice, and I heard the light patter of small canine feet inside.

"Out here," I called.

I did not turn from watching the white wolf as Maggie and her Bichon Frise, Louie, joined us on the back deck. Frank dropped into a crouch to greet the smaller dog.

"I came as soon as I could," Maggie said. I turned to her when she placed a hand on my shoulder. "Are you alright?"

"Do you see the wolf there across the river?"

Her gaze moved past me, and even in the moonlight I could see the wrinkle in her brow. "What wolf?"

I scanned the far shore. The riverbank was empty.

I was certain I was not experiencing supernatural visions. I had not ruled out the possibility that I was going insane.

"Are you drunk?" she asked quietly.

"Not drunk enough," I admitted.

I tucked the box under my arm and led her back into the inn, locking the french doors behind us. The dogs followed us through the sunroom into the kitchen.

Maggie watched me warily as I placed the box on the table and pulled out a chair for her. She searched my face as she sat across from me. "Is this about the girl?"

"No," I said. "This is…This is about something else."

Her gaze dropped to the box, and her throat worked. "Do you have any of that whiskey I can smell on you left? I think I need some before you tell me what's in that box."

"You do," I agreed. I stood and retrieved the bottle from the cupboard. I did not bother with a glass. I handed her the bottle.

"Did they find Winona or Emma?" she whispered.

I took the seat across from her again. "Winona."

She nodded and took a long drink of whiskey. When she stretched her hand across the table, I captured it in mine. Her grip was strong and tight.

My head throbbed in time with the whine of the miter saw the next morning.

The River Inn was a sprawling cabin of roughhewn timber and glass. When Faye Anders purchased it four years ago, it had been decrepit. After she remodeled the interior and opened it to visitors, the inn remained full from March until October.

Faye had done a solid job renovating the rooms, but a look of dereliction still clung to the exterior. It was worn and weathered, desperately in need of a handyman.

After attacking Senator Grant Larson and breaking his jaw, I had been fired from the police force. I knew I was lucky not to have been charged with assault, but I had been bored out of my mind within three days. I had more time on my hands than I had since I was fourteen years old. The only time I had no job and too much time was when I had been laid up for a year after a bull had crushed me into an arena floor. I spent four months being pieced back together and then eight months relearning how to walk.

Bitterness festered quickly in those weeks and months of idleness and pain, unable to do anything but lie in bed and think about how life as I knew it was over. Winona had been a constant, sleeping contorted in a chair beside my hospital bed, clenching my hand in hers as I grimaced and sweated my way through physical therapy and rehabilitation.

As a constant, she had taken the full brunt of my anger and frustration. I did not know why she had remained with me for those fifteen years we had together. I did not know why I had been so adamant about driving her away.

Now, I had no one to rail against, though I felt that same simmer of frustration coursing through me. Maggie told me once that I was a man who needed an obsession. She was not wrong.

Over the last few months, I had thrown all of my frustration into swinging a hammer, focusing on the inn. I had worked on the roof, put in new doors, and repaired the listing bottom step leading up to the wraparound porch. Now I had moved on to replacing all of the shutters.

Movement caught the corner of my eye, but I did not glance up until I finished cutting a board to length. I straightened, released the switch on the saw, and took my safety goggles off as I turned.

"What do you want?"

Frank sat up from his sprawl on the front porch at

my voice. When he spotted our visitor, he bounded off the steps and loped to the kid standing at the edge of the drive. She backed up quickly and held her hands out to the approaching poodle.

"Easy, easy," she said. There was a nervous tremor in her voice.

I sighed and rubbed the back of my neck. "He won't hurt you."

She held herself tensely as the poodle sniffed her outstretched hands.

"Frank," I called. "Come here." He trotted back to my side, and I would have sworn he wore an expression of bafflement at the concept of anyone being frightened of him.

The girl sagged slightly and hitched her backpack higher on her shoulders. "So, what are you doing?"

She's someone's little girl. Ed's words echoed in my head. She was someone's daughter, but she was not mine. Even so, I felt myself softening toward her. "Making board and batten shutters for the windows."

She approached me slowly. Her careful movements and watchful gaze reminded me of a wild animal. "That's cool. Can I help?"

In the morning light, I thought she might be younger than I first suspected, closer to fifteen than twenty.

Several years ago, a TV special had covered missing children. Emma had been one of the children picked for the show, and artists had rendered a drawing of what she could look like now, fifteen years after her disappearance. I refused to look at the composite sketch. Emma remained in my mind as she had been just days before her second birthday. It did me no good to wonder about the features of a little girl who had not been allowed to grow up.

But studying the girl before me now, I found myself wondering what Emma would have been like at this age. I wondered if I would have remained as distant with her as a teen as I had been when she was a toddler.

I knew nothing about children. They had never interested me, and Winona and I had never talked about having them. Until the day she told me she was pregnant. I had been prepared to tell her I wanted a divorce. We had plenty of years between us to prove I was not husband material. From the moment Winona showed me the positive result on the pregnancy test, Emma had felt like a ball and chain around my neck.

"I don't have to help if it's going to bother you," the kid before me said.

Her face was tight, clenched against the blow of rejection. I recognized the expression. It was not that different on this girl's face as it had been on my daughter's years ago.

"It's not going to bother me." I was as surprised as she was to hear the words come out of my mouth. I nodded to the second work bench I had set up. "You can start priming and painting the boards I cut."

With her focus now on the stack of boards, she crossed the lawn more readily, the tightness in her expression easing. "Should we put them together first?"

She did not take her backpack off as she grabbed a hammer from my toolkit and popped the lid off of the paint can.

"Nope," I said. "Easier to do it before I assemble the shutters."

I watched her stir the paint and pour a portion into a tray. She moved confidently without spilling a drop. I donned my safety glasses and turned back to the miter saw.

"Is this what you're doing now that you're not a police officer any longer?" she asked.

I paused, hand on the saw's switch. "How did you know I was a police officer?"

She was silent, and when I glanced over my shoulder, her head was down and she was focused on moving the paint roller over the board. Her shrug was carefully noncommittal, but she did not look at me. "I must have heard it at the diner."

She had not, I knew that for a fact. Those in the diner who had witnessed her interaction with Ed and Betty had accepted her for whom she claimed to be. A steady stream had come by the table to hug her and shake Ed's hand. They pointedly ignored me as they exclaimed over Emma's return. None had mentioned their suspicions that I had killed my wife and daughter, and none had spoken of my previous employment.

I did not correct the girl, though. She had obviously done her research on me.

We worked without speaking. Frank returned to his sprawl on the front porch. The saw whined, and sawdust soon coated my forearms. When I had finished cutting the boards to size, I grabbed the ladder and moved around the house, taking down the dilapidated shutters.

"I finished painting," the girl said.

I looked down to see her at the foot of the ladder.

"Is there more I can help with?" she asked.

I tossed the shutter I had just removed into the growing pile and climbed down the ladder. "How did you get here?"

She thrust a thumb over her shoulder in the direction of downtown. "I walked from Ed and Betty's."

"How did you get to Raven's Gap?" I asked. "How did you find me?"

"It's…" She crossed her arms. She avoided my gaze when she said, "It's kind of a long story."

"Give me the short version."

She scuffed a foot in the dirt and stared at her shoes for a long moment before looking directly at me. "I took a Greyhound from Denver to Cheyenne, and I hitchhiked from there."

"You're from Denver?"

"No." She hitched her backpack higher on her shoulders. "I'm from Pine Ridge."

"You're Oglala Lakota," I said.

She hesitated, expression frozen. "Yes."

Winona had been Hunkpapa Lakota, though I did not share this with the girl before me. "I have some exterior silicone caulk to fill these old holes," I said. "You want to come behind me and fill these holes from the old shutters while the paint is drying?"

The tension left her face, and she nodded. "I can do that."

"Good," I said softly. "Get busy, kid."

She darted a smile in my direction and hurried to retrieve the caulk gun.

I rubbed the back of my neck. That she had secrets was obvious. That she was not ready to give up the charade of being Emma yet was also obvious.

Seven

ANNIE

I meant to tell him the truth.

I had awakened to the smell of bacon and coffee. When I wandered downstairs, I found Ed and Betty in the kitchen preparing breakfast. A place was set at the table for me.

I meant to tell them the truth, but the words were stuck in my throat. My stomach growled loudly, and I felt my face flush.

Breakfast was a quiet affair. Ed's eyes were red-rimmed, and Betty's face looked more gaunt today than it had yesterday. I wanted to ask them if they were okay, but I was afraid I had caused their sorrow.

When we finished eating, I said, "I can clean up."

"You don't need to do that," Betty said.

"I'd like to," I insisted.

She touched my hand as Ed pushed back from the table. He bent and kissed the top of my head and then did the same for his wife.

"I'm headed to the shop," he said, and gestured toward the front of the house. "The mechanic shop across the lane is mine. I'll be there if you need me."

Despite my protests, Betty helped me clear the table and wash the dishes from our meal. When we were finished, she paused beside me. She placed her hand on my cheek and peered into my eyes.

I searched her gaze. *Tell her*, I thought. *Just tell her*. The words were there, caught behind my tongue.

"I'm going to lie down for a bit," Betty said.

"Are you okay?" I asked.

She patted my cheek, her worn palm gentle. "No," she said softly. "I'm dying."

I caught her wrist in my hands. "*What?*"

"Cancer. I've had it for a while."

I barely knew this woman, but I felt the words like a blow to my chest. "Can they…Is there something they can do?" My gaze went to her head, covered by a decorative scarf. I had guessed she was ill, but I had not grasped the severity.

"They've tried. My body can't fight it any longer. And…" Her gaze moved past me, and her stare took on a blank quality for a long moment before she focused again on me. "And I'm tired."

Tears burned my eyes. What had I done? I'd told a dying woman I was her long-lost granddaughter.

"I'm sorry," I whispered.

Her other hand came up, and she cupped my face in her palms. Her gaze sharpened. "You don't need to be." Her voice was so firm, her eyes so direct, that for an instant, I thought she knew. She turned away, and her steps were slow. "I'll be in my room if you need anything."

I slumped into a chair at the kitchen table and stared

blindly through the window at the stretch of woods behind the house. I was used to wide open spaces, being able to see all the way to the horizon. At the moment, in this wooded valley, unable to see the sky, I felt caged and claustrophobic.

I shoved back from the table and hurried up the stairs. In the bedroom, I dropped to my knees beside the bed and pulled my backpack from its hiding place. I took the steps three at a time on the way down.

Outside, I sucked in a deep breath, tilting my head back to see the sky. It remained where it always was. I stared upward, neck craned, until that tight, hot knot in my chest eased.

It was wildfire season. I could smell it in the air, though the wind was still today. I could see a good stretch of Raven's Gap from my vantage point in front of Ed and Betty's home. It was not a large town. Most of the hotels, tourist shops, and restaurants were off of the state road.

I had studied every map I could find of the area when I first heard of Raven's Gap in January. The town was built on a hill, laid out on a grid across three streets running parallel up the hill to Main Street and three streets running perpendicular across those. The local businesses were largely housed in old brick and timber buildings that looked like they had been here since the town was founded. It was like stepping back in time, and I half expected to see horses along the street instead of cars.

Unease nipped at my heels like a wild dog. I needed to tell the truth.

The inn was not far from here. I tightened the straps

of my backpack and crossed the street, winding between houses as I made my way to the eastern edge of town. I could hear the river well before I could see it. I could also hear the buzz of a saw as I moved through a stretch of woods.

I stepped from between the trees and stared across the street at the inn. Hector was out front feeding boards through a round saw.

He was a lot more intimidating than I thought he would be. He had been abrupt and no-nonsense on the news interviews I had seen on tv. The camera had not captured how gruff and dismissive he was, though.

I swallowed and crossed the street. I needed him on my side, but I was afraid I had ruined everything. I just needed to tell him the truth.

When he turned and glared at me, though, the words evaporated. He would tell me to get lost. He would refuse to help me if he knew I was not his Emma. He didn't seem to have much patience for me even thinking I was his daughter.

He surprised me by allowing me to work alongside him, though. I messed up by letting it slip that I knew he had been a police officer and then admitting I was from Pine Ridge. I thought he would be a typical white man and not know the difference in the tribes. He had not pressed the issue, though. Maybe Lakota was Lakota to him.

I focused on painting the boards for the shutters flawlessly and then caulking the holes from the old shutters neatly and quickly. I liked the work. It gave my hands something to do.

"Nice job," Hector said.

I turned to find him standing behind me. His gaze was not on my work, though, but on me. I had the uncomfortable sense that the man could see straight through me and knew I lied.

"I can help with more," I said. I needed the man to like me and not turn me away once he knew the truth.

I expected him to refuse. He was silent for several moments, and that big white dog of his came trotting over to lean against his leg.

I forced myself not to take a quick step back. I had been bitten by a dog when I was younger. All I could remember of the incident was how massive the animal had been over me when it knocked me to the ground, how hot its breath had been, and how it felt like my skin was tearing from the bone when it bit my calf. I still had the series of scars on my leg from its teeth.

"Come back tomorrow," Hector said suddenly.

I blinked and realized I had been staring blindly at the dog beside him. The poodle's head was tilted, and he studied me with a gaze that seemed almost human.

"The boards will be dry," Hector continued. "You can help me put the shutters together."

"I'll be here in the morning first thing," I said, and I could not keep the eagerness from my voice.

He studied me for a long moment, and I forced myself not to look away from his gaze. "You comfortable at Ed and Betty's?" he asked suddenly.

"Yes," I said. The thought of the older couple made my throat tight. "They've been nothing but kind to me."

"That's how they would treat their granddaughter," he said.

His gaze did not leave mine as he said the words,

and I swallowed. Did he know?

"I..." My throat was dry.

His eyes narrowed, and it made his face look harder and colder than it already did. I lost my nerve.

"I should be going. I didn't tell them I was coming over here, and I don't want them to worry."

He said nothing, merely watched me as I backed away and put the caulk gun on the work bench.

"I'll be back tomorrow," I said. I turned and hurried up the drive of the inn.

At the road, I glanced back and found Hector standing where I left him, staring after me. I looked away quickly and strode down the sidewalk.

"Stupid, stupid, stupid," I muttered to myself. I was an idiot.

I crossed the street and cut through the woods to head back into town. Once through the woods, I moved down the street toward Ed's shop. A metallic groan of brakes brought my head up. I glanced back and saw a car ease away from the curb at the end of the road.

It was moving slowly, and the windshield was so darkly tinted I could not see the driver. There was no crosswalk, but I hurried across the street.

Tires squealed. I froze halfway across the pavement, gaze locked on the car suddenly bearing down on me. It veered from its lane and straddled the line painted down the center of the street. The vehicle raced straight toward me.

Shock and fear held me in its grip for excruciating moments. I could hear my own breaths. Then with a jolt, the paralysis released its grip on me. I dove to the side, my palms and knees taking the brunt of the impact when I hit the ground. The engine revved, and the car sped past so close to me I could feel the heat of it. With a squeal of tires, it turned the corner and was gone as quickly as it had raced toward me.

I stayed huddled in the gutter, heart beating in my throat, trying to make sense of what had just happened. The driver had to have seen me. There was no way to miss seeing me. Someone had tried to run me over. Someone had attempted to deliberately hit me with their car.

I started to shake.

"Hey!"

My head jerked up. The woman from the diner hurried toward me. Her face was tight with concern.

"Are you alright?" she asked as she reached me. She knelt beside me and placed a hand on my shoulder.

I could not help leaning into her touch. "That car just tried to run me over," I said, voice trembling.

"Did you see what kind of car it was? Who was driving?" She pulled her phone out of her pocket.

"No!" I grabbed her hand. Her gaze flew to mine, and I immediately pulled back. "Don't call the police. It's fine. I'm sure it was an accident," I lied. "Probably texting and driving."

She studied my face. Again, I was reminded of a hawk's perceptive gaze. "Are you hurt?" she finally asked.

I stood, grimacing as I brushed at my knees. "I'm okay." My palms were scraped raw, and there were pieces of gravel embedded in my torn knees.

"Come on," she said. "I have a first aid kit in my

office at the diner."

I followed her the few blocks to the diner. She stopped in the doorway to the kitchen and spoke briefly to her staff before leading me down the hall into her office.

She gestured to her couch, where a fluffy white dog was curled up. He sat up, tail wagging so hard his whole body swayed. This dog was more my size. He couldn't rip your leg apart or kill you.

"Who's this?" I asked. I sat down, and the little dog promptly climbed in my lap and stood on his hind legs to try to lick my chin. I laughed and held him away from me.

"That's Louie," she said as she collected the first aid kit from a drawer in her desk. She pulled her chair around her desk and sat in front of me. When she held out her hand, I placed mine in her palm and watched her face closely. She wiped my torn skin with an alcohol pad and then applied a liberal smear of ointment before smoothing a bandage in place.

Her face was calm and expressionless, and her hands were calloused but gentle.

"It's Maggie, right?" I asked. "I think I heard Hector call you that."

"Yes," she said, but she didn't offer anything else.

Silence fell between us as she finished bandaging my hands and moved to my knees. Louie abandoned his effort to lick my face and curled up in my lap.

"You don't like me very much, do you?" I finally asked.

Maggie paused and then resumed picking the gravel from my knees. She was quiet for several long minutes.

I thought she was going to ignore my question.

"Winona Lewis was my closest friend," she said eventually, "and now Hector is. I was with her in the hospital when she was giving birth because Hector was working a shift at the police department. I thought I would have the chance to be there for every big moment in her life, in her daughter's." Her voice caught. She looked up and met my gaze. I swallowed. "I care about Ed and Betty, about Jack. This entire town turned out to help search for Winona and Emma. Everyone in Raven's Gap mourned both of them and blamed Hector for their disappearance. And everyone here has spent fifteen years hoping that one day both of them would return home."

I couldn't hold her gaze any longer. I focused on my fingers as I stroked Louie's head.

"I don't think you realize the magnitude of the blow you are dealing to so many people," she said, and though her voice was low, her tone was hard. "You've reminded me of all those moments I was robbed of, because someone stole Winona and Emma from us." She fell silent again. After several moments, she said, "In answer to your question, no, I don't dislike you. I just don't trust you."

There was nothing I could say except a whispered, "I'm sorry."

She nodded and focused again on my knees. "I don't trust you, but I'm hoping you won't hurt the people I care about."

"I won't," I assured her. "I don't want to hurt anyone."

"Good." She packed away her first aid kit and stood. "Then you need to tell the truth sooner rather than later. You're not Emma, and you're only hurting people by claiming you are."

"I just..." Louie rolled over in my lap, and I scratched his belly. Focusing on the dog allowed me to tell her the truth. "Now that I've said I'm Emma, I don't know how to tell them I'm not. I really *don't* want to hurt anyone. I didn't...I didn't mean to say I was Emma."

"Let me tell you something that will make it a bit easier," she said. I looked up at her, and her voice gentled. "They already know you're not Emma."

"Are you sure?" I asked. "Ed and Betty...they've been so good to me."

She reached out and placed a finger on my brow. "Emma fell into a cabinet when she was learning how to walk. She needed ten stitches just here."

"Oh."

"The rest of the town may not know the truth, but from the moment they met you, Hector, Ed, and Betty did."

"Then why...?" My voice trailed off.

"Why have Ed and Betty taken you in?"

I nodded. "They've treated me like I *am* Emma."

"That's just the type of people they are."

"Is that why...?" I hesitated. I still did not know what the extent of this woman's relationship was with Hector.

"Is that why what?" she prompted.

"Is that why Hector is kind of a jerk?"

She startled me by throwing back her head and laughing. "No, honey," she said when she finally had control of herself again. "I'm afraid being a jerk is just who he is."

I wasn't certain if that made me feel better or not.

She must have seen the uncertainty on my face, because she sobered. "If you need his help, just tell him."

"What if he won't?" I whispered. "There's no one else who can help me."

She searched my face and finally said, "I have a feeling Hector won't turn you away."

I gently deposited Louie on the couch beside me and gave his head one last stroke. "Thank you." My palms and knees were sore and throbbing with heat.

"If he does..." Maggie's voice stopped me in the doorway. I turned back to her. "If he does turn you away, let me know. I'll talk to him."

I left the diner feeling lighter.

As soon as I stepped outside, though, a light flashed and a microphone was thrust in my face.

"Emma Lewis, can you tell us where you've been for the last fifteen years?" a man asked.

"Were you being held against your will, Emma?" a woman called.

I staggered backward.

"What has your reunion been like with your family?"

"Emma, has your father insisted on a paternity test?"

"Did you know your mother's remains have been found? Is this timing related?"

There were news reporters everywhere. Another light flashed, and I threw a hand up to shield my eyes.

"Emma!"

The voices came from all directions. I shoved my way through the crowd. Lights flashed, and several microphones hit me in the chin and cheek as they were pushed into my face.

I had wings for feet. I always had. Running was the one thing that emptied my mind of all the things that ate at me. Before I had dropped out of school, I had been the sole member of the track team. I won every race I had run in competitions with other schools. For a time, I thought it had been my escape route. Until I realized sometimes there was just no escaping.

But now, I ran.

Eight

HECTOR

My phone rang, and the number listed on the screen was the police department's.

"It's me," Joan Marsden said softly when I answered. Her voice was as fine and polished as the rest of her.

Our affair had been going on for ten years now. She only showed up on my doorstep when her husband began using his fists. There was no set schedule. Sometimes she had been in my bed several nights a week; other times it was months before I saw her outside of the police department, where she worked the front desk. It always perplexed me that she came to me, of all men, for gentleness, but I gave it to her as best I could.

I had only seen her once since moving to the inn. My property outside of town was a place she could slip away to unnoticed, but there would be plenty of talk in town if she started showing up at the inn. Instead, when she called me last month, I had met her at a hotel in Gardiner.

She never called me from the police station's line.

"What's wrong?" I asked.

"You'll need to come to the station. Emma's fine," she said, and it felt as if a stone had been dropped in my gut. "She's here with me. But the press is outside."

"Shit. I'll be right there."

Frank leapt to his feet as soon as I stood and trotted at my heels as I left the inn and headed to my truck.

It only took me a few minutes to reach the police department. It was swarmed with news vans. The press milled around the front entrance. The sight of the vultures circling tightened my gut. They had dogged my steps for the first months after Winona and Emma's disappearance. At first, they had been courteous and sympathetic when I was just a husband and father. Once I was a suspect, though, they had been ruthless.

I waited for Frank to leap to the ground and then slammed the door. Several of the reporters glanced over at me and did a double take. I could see the murmur that spread through the crowd. Then, as one, the group turned and hurried toward me.

Frank growled.

"Easy," I reminded him quietly.

"Hector? Hector Lewis?"

I did not respond to the impatient queries.

"Hector, how are you dealing with the discovery of your wife's remains?"

"Can you confirm your daughter has been found?"

They hurled the questions at me as I pushed my way through the crowd. They parted around me and steered well clear of Frank's bared teeth.

One woman shoved a microphone in my face, and I was forced to halt. "Mr. Lewis, given that you were a suspect in your wife and daughter's disappearance, how does this change things for you?"

Winona had been born and raised here. She had known everyone by name, worked at Thornton's Market when Carl Thornton's father still ran it, and returned home to their welcoming embrace after a short but successful career as a barrel racer. She had been their bright star, their golden girl. I had always been the stranger she brought home with her. The one who had crushed other men's dreams of making her theirs, the one who had dampened her smile and tinged her laugh with unhappiness.

After she was gone, I was much more than that. Even the police suspected I was responsible for her disappearance. I had stopped defending myself years ago.

This changed nothing. People would still think what they wanted.

The woman pushed the microphone at me, and I had to suppress the urge to shove it away.

I met her gaze. "No comment."

Whatever she heard in my voice or saw in my eyes had her rethinking her bulldog approach. She pulled back enough for me to move around her.

No one followed us across the barrier of the sliding glass entrance into the police department.

I turned the corner in the lobby. I no longer had a badge to let myself through the locked door, but Joan pushed the door open as I approached.

With the cameras all over the station, her touch on my arm was strictly professional. "I saw them hounding her," she said quietly. Frank leaned against her legs, sighing when she stroked his ears. "When she ran past, I flagged her down and brought her inside."

I looked past her and took in the girl. She was perched on the edge of a chair, hands tucked under her legs. She swiveled the chair back and forth. The trepidation was clear on her face. She looked like the child she was, all bluster and bravado shorn away.

"Thank you, Joan."

She nodded and glanced over her shoulder at the girl. "I can't believe she's alive, after all these years. You must be so happy."

"I must be," I echoed.

The girl stood when I turned to her. She crossed her arms over her chest and clutched the straps of her ever-present backpack.

"Let's get you out of here," I said.

We were swarmed as soon as we stepped outside. When the girl pressed close to me, ducking her head against me, I automatically wrapped my arm around her narrow shoulders and pulled her to my side as I steered us through the crowd.

I ignored the questions hurled our way and refused to look into the cameras pointed in our direction.

"Emma!" a man shouted and thrust his microphone in the girl's face, almost clipping her cheek. "Tell us—"

I caught the microphone in a tight grip. The reporter jerked, startled.

"Get that fucking thing out of her face or you'll eat it," I snapped.

He scowled. "Look—"

A commotion behind us caught his attention. I glanced back to see Joan exit the station and direct that perfect smile at the gathered crowd. "Ladies and gentlemen, the chief will be holding a press conference tomorrow morning. He'll be out in the next fifteen minutes to announce the time."

Frank leapt into the truck as soon as I opened the door, and the girl scrambled over the driver's seat after him. She was silent as I turned the key in the ignition. I had to loosen my grip on the steering wheel and make sure I did not burn rubber as I left the parking lot. I kept an eye on the rearview mirror to see if anyone followed us.

"I'm sorry," she said, voice subdued. "I didn't think about…" Her voice trailed away. I spared her a glance and found her staring out the window. "I didn't think."

There were repercussions for claiming to be my missing daughter, but I had not anticipated the press getting wind of her. I wondered who had talked about her arrival in town.

"Don't worry about it," I said.

Silence fell between us as I traversed the few blocks to Ed and Betty's. I stopped at the crossroad when I caught sight of the news vans parked on the street in front of the house.

"Oh no," she whispered. "I didn't mean to cause trouble for them."

I caught sight of Jack's truck in their driveway. "They'll be fine," I assured her.

Vultures was all too apt a term. I turned down the next street to avoid being seen and cut through town to the inn. My presence there was known in town, but all records still listed the burnt stretch of meadow where my Airstream once stood as my residence.

There were no reporters parked on the inn's lawn, so I pulled into the drive and parked.

"You can stay here for the night," I said. "I'll let Ed and Betty know."

She and Frank followed me inside.

There were guests in the great room, but no one spared us a second glance. Evelyn was in the kitchen, though, and her brows went up when she caught sight of the girl.

"Hello." She glanced back and forth between us.

"This is my daughter, Emma." The words felt as if they caught in my throat, but my voice was even as I spoke. From the corner of my eye, I saw the girl glance quickly at me. "Emma, this is Evelyn. She runs the inn and works at the museum in town."

If ever a woman fit the old adage of *still waters run deep*, Evelyn certainly did. I had a feeling a lot went on beneath the surface that she never allowed to show. I still wondered if she had played a role in the disappearance of the man who had stalked her for a year when she lived in Atlanta. The five-year-old case had grown cold.

Even though I had been wrong about Jeff Roosevelt killing my wife and daughter fifteen years ago, he had proven himself to be a dangerous predator. She and I had been the only ones who had seen it. And she had been the one to end the serial killer's spree.

At the moment, she did not even bat an eyelash over the supposed identity of the girl at my side. "It's nice to meet you."

"You too," the girl said softly.

Evelyn stared at me for a long moment, and then she turned to the girl and smiled. "I'm making supper. Nothing fancy, just a meatloaf. You both are welcome to join me."

Evelyn and I were not friends. We lived around one another, sharing our space but not our time. I wondered what she saw in the girl that made her extend the offer.

"Sure," I said.

"I can help you," the girl offered.

"First, let me show you where you can stay tonight," I told her. I looked to Evelyn. "Reporters may show up at the door."

She grimaced. "I'll take care of it if they do."

The girl followed me down the hall to the rooms I now called home. The far corner of the inn was set up like an efficiency apartment. The furniture remained from the last inhabitants: the sofa, coffee table, and television in the living room; the child's bedroom on the other side of the bathroom that adjoined the two rooms. The only changes I had made were in the bedroom I slept in.

The girl's brow wrinkled in confusion as she took in the bedroom, the Legos and train set in the corner, the patterned sheets on the bed. "Whose room was this?" she asked.

"A child's," I said. A little boy who was living a far better, safer life having been kidnapped than he would have otherwise. "A woman and her son lived here before me."

"You didn't change the rooms?" Curiosity was evident in her face and voice as she wandered into the room.

"Not this one," I said. "You're my first guest."

She moved to the door leading into the bathroom

that adjoined the bedrooms. She closed and locked it, testing the handle once the door was locked. I could tell the action was automatic. When she glanced over her shoulder and found me watching her, she hurried glanced away and opened the door with all the studied nonchalance of a child who had been caught doing something she did not want someone to see.

"This is great," she said. "Thank you."

I did not like the implications of her caution, and I was not certain why the idea that she was frightened and in danger was beginning to bother me so much.

Nine

ANNIE

I put all of my strength into helping my grandmother off the floor where she had fallen.

We were both breathing hard by the time I got her back into bed. I tucked the quilts tightly around her.

"I'll stay home with you," I told her.

She shook her head. "I'm fine. I just got a little dizzy when I stood." She glanced past me and forced a smile to her trembling lips.

I glanced over my shoulder and found Kimi standing in the doorway. Her eyes were wide and frightened.

I turned back to my grandmother. She clutched my hand, but her grip was weak. She held my gaze. "I'm fine. Take your sister to school."

I swallowed and nodded. I caught Kimi's hand in my own and led her from the room.

She was silent as I made sure her backpack was packed. There was a single slice of bread left. I cut off the mold growing on one corner of the crust. I managed to scrape enough peanut butter from the empty jar to spread the thinnest layer across the bread.

My stomach growled, but I folded the bread, tucked it

in a bag, and placed it in Kimi's backpack for her lunch.

Her hand clung to mine as we walked the long miles to school. She usually jabbered endlessly about her kindergarten class, her friends, the shape of the clouds, anything that came to mind. She was never silent, and it made my heart beat too fast in my chest. I told her about the book we were reading in my fourth grade class to fill the quiet as we walked.

"I'm scared, Annie," she said suddenly, voice small.

I swallowed. I was scared, too, but I couldn't tell her that.

"You don't need to be," I said, and I had to hide all of my own fear from my voice.

"Unci..."

"Unci is going to be okay." I said it to reassure myself, too, even though I was afraid it was a lie.

She sniffled, and I tightened my grip on her hand.

"I'm always going to be here for you. You don't ever have to be scared, because I'll always take care of you."

"Promise?"

I freed my hand from hers so I could wrap it around her shoulders. "I promise."

I lurched out of sleep with a strangled gasp. My face was damp, and I struggled upright, scrubbing the tears from my cheeks.

I glanced at the door leading into the bathroom and then the opposite door. I had locked both before climbing in bed, and the doorknobs remained still.

I pressed the heels of my hands against my eyes, sucking in an uneven breath. I had broken that promise.

The horror of finding her was just as bad as the horror of having to leave her in that dirty, flea-bitten hotel room. *Jane Doe* was what the police report would read, and that bothered me more than anything.

She had always been able to pass for white. Maybe that would make the police dig a little deeper into what happened instead of them just writing it off as another dead American Indian girl with no name.

I wondered again if that was what had become of my mother. If her body lay on a slab in a morgue somewhere with the tag on her toe reading *Jane Doe*. She had never returned home from leaving in the middle of the night to get medicine for Kimi. Holding me in her arms one moment, and gone the next, as if she had never even existed.

She had, though, and I collected my memories of her and clung to them with everything I had. After ten years, they were worn and faded around the edges, but I wouldn't lose the only thing I had left of her. The memory of how cool her hands always were and how warm her hair felt around me when we slept in her bed. Now that I was older, I wondered if she was unhappy, if she was lonely, if she ever felt anything but exhaustion when she worked numerous jobs to keep us fed. But all I could remember was her smile, how she never said no when I asked her to play.

She was the reason I knew about Raven's Gap. As soon as the news broke about the serial killer and the mass grave of Native women, I had called the number on the screen and offered my DNA for comparison. Hope was a cruel creature, a true trickster. None of the women found were my mother.

I swallowed hard against the anger and bitterness

that tightened my throat. I threw the covers off me. I needed air. I crept from my room, wincing when a floorboard in the living room creaked underfoot. I glanced back at Hector's room, but the door remained closed and the seam showed no light on in the room.

The inn was dark and silent around me as I moved through the kitchen and a pretty sunroom into the great room. The moon spilled through the huge windows along the back wall. I almost ran to the doors leading out onto the deck, but I stumbled to a halt when I pushed them open and saw I was not the only one who needed air.

Hector sat in one of those chairs with a deeply curved seat. His boots were propped up on the railing, and his dog was sprawled on the deck at his side. Frank sat up when he heard the door open, and his tail began to thump when he spotted me.

Hector did not turn to look at me. I thought he might be asleep. I started to retreat back into the inn, when he suddenly said, "Pull up a chair, kid."

I grabbed a deck chair and dragged it beside his. When I sank down in the chair, I mimicked his posture with my feet up on the railing.

It was a warm night, but the breeze carried the scent of smoke and the sky in the southeast gleamed with a distant fire. The river sang as it swept past.

I glanced at Hector from the corner of my eye when he remained silent. In the dark, I couldn't make out his expression. I remembered the questions the reporters had thrown at us earlier.

"Was it true?" I asked. "What they said about my…?" I couldn't keep up the charade when my own mother was so fresh in my mind. "About your wife? She's been found?"

"Yes."

"What…?" I bit my lip. Could I even ask this? "What happened to her?"

He was silent for so long I thought he wouldn't answer, but finally he said, "There was a double blow to her head." His voice was remote and cold. "The coroner thinks she was struck on the back of the head and then fell and hit her temple."

I swallowed. I had always hoped that my mother didn't suffer. That she was not raped and tortured before her death, that whoever had killed her had done so quickly and painlessly. I had no doubt she was dead. If she had been alive, she would have fought her way back to us.

"What about…?" Maggie had told me he already knew, that all I needed to do was tell the truth. In the darkness, it seemed a little easier to force the words past my throat. "What about your daughter?"

He didn't react to the words for several heartbeats. I held my breath. This was when he would throw me out and tell me to get lost.

"She's still missing," he said.

I turned my head to see him clearly. I wondered what kind of dad he had been, if he had been a nicer, softer man before his wife and daughter disappeared. I would tell him everything, I decided. Right now. My name, how I had been familiar with Raven's Gap—and with him—for months, what had happened to my sister, why I needed him.

I took a deep breath and turned to face him.

"Something on your mind?" he asked.

His voice was mild, but he didn't look at me. His gaze was fixed, and when I followed its direction, I sat up, pushing myself to the edge of the chair, and stared.

"That's a white wolf," I breathed, no louder than a whisper for fear of frightening the wolf standing on the opposite bank of the river.

Her head came up suddenly, and I could have sworn she looked directly at me.

I had never had the honor of seeing a wolf. They had long been driven out of existence in South Dakota. The coyote were in abundance, but even though I had heard tales of wolves occasionally passing through the area, I had never seen one outside of photographs.

She was majestic. Power and grace, loyalty and ruthlessness wrapped in gorgeous pure white fur.

Hector's boots dropped to the deck. He leaned forward, elbows on his knees, and glanced back and forth between the wolf and me.

"A white wolf revealed herself to you?" I whispered, and I couldn't deny the awe I felt. She had allowed me to see her, too. My heart leapt as if it wanted to race alongside the wolf.

"You can see her, too?" Hector asked. There was something in his voice I did not understand.

My gaze darted away from him and back to the wolf. She stood like a spirit in the darkness. She would have been one with the night if not for her coloring.

"I can see her," I said. "She's the most beautiful thing I've ever seen."

When Hector remained quiet, my gaze was drawn back to him. I felt my eyes widen. He wasn't looking at me any longer. His eyes were locked on the white wolf, and he was smiling.

Ten

HECTOR

Winona's skull sat on the table beside my bed. It was the first thing I saw when I opened my eyes.

The gray light just before dawn filtered into the room. I reached out and cupped the dome of her skull in my hand, feeling the depression at the back against my palm.

When I had allowed myself to ponder the possibility, I had wondered if Winona had sent me the white wolf. Whether she was a guide or a messenger, I did not know. I only knew she haunted my steps more often than not and no one else had seen her.

Winona had been Lakota. It was not my culture, but the beliefs of the American Indians were something I had been in close contact with through my wife. I knew they viewed nature and its creatures from a different perspective, one filled with spirits and rich with meaning.

I had come to accept that perhaps the white wolf only existed in my mind, but then the kid had seen her as well.

"Is she for both of us?" I asked the skull quietly.

Frank was sprawled across my feet, and his head came up at the sound of my voice. The remains of my wife offered no response.

I pushed out of bed. In the bathroom, I glanced at the door leading into the adjoining bedroom and remembered the careful way the girl had checked for a lock when I had shown her the room.

I wandered from the apartment into the inn's kitchen several minutes later and found Evelyn standing at the sink. She nursed a cup of coffee, staring out over the river.

"She watches you," she said quietly without turning away from the view. Frank leaned against her legs, and she stroked his ears. "She looks at you like she wants to speak, but she doesn't know how to find the words." Her gaze slid to me. "You look at her in the same way."

I filled a mug and noticed my phone on the counter. I had forgotten and left it there last night. I powered up the screen and noticed I had a number of missed calls from the police department. "It's…complicated."

She made a noncommittal noise. "Isn't it always?"

I listened to one of the voicemails left on my phone and swore under my breath.

"Trouble?" Evelyn asked.

"Isn't there always?" I said, echoing her words. I checked the date on my phone and saw it was Saturday. "Are you going to be around the inn today?"

"All day," she confirmed.

"When you see…" I had to force the name past my lips. "When you see Emma, will you ask her to stay here at the inn and not go out until I get back? The news crews are still lurking around town."

"Sure, I'll tell her."

I drained my coffee mug and looked at Frank. "Ready?"

He abandoned his lean against Evelyn and followed me to my truck.

Several news vans were parked in front of the police department when we arrived. No one called after us, though, as Frank and I crossed the lot and entered the lobby.

Joan was behind the front desk, and she hit the button to grant me access to the hall as soon as she saw me. She met me as I pushed through the door into the corridor.

She spared me a smile and handed Frank a treat from the jar she kept at her desk. "You got my messages?"

"Just a few minutes ago," I said. "Is the chief here yet?"

She nodded. "He's in the conference room. You can go on back. I'll let him know you're on the way."

It was a strange sensation, walking the halls of the station once more. I had joined the police department thirty years ago for a lack of anything better to do. At thirty years of age, I had a wife I was not entirely certain I wanted anymore who had been keen to move back to her hometown as soon as my career on the circuit was over. I had a new knee, hip, and shoulder courtesy of a bull, and I was fresh from rehab with a piss-poor attitude and a bitterness wedged deep inside my gut at the turn life had taken.

At thirty, I was young and angry and stupid. When

I saw the ad in the newspaper, I thought, *Why the hell not?* I had nothing better to do.

I had spent half my life as a police officer. I did not miss it in the least.

Donald Marsden, the chief, was not alone in the conference room. Grover Westland, the county coroner, was with him, along with the department's commander and the Park County sheriff.

"Hector." Donald stood. "I'm glad you got the message I had Joan leave for you."

The chief was a man who was very proud of having been a Marine and found endless opportunities to tell people so. He liked to label himself a Vietnam War combat veteran when I knew for a fact he had never been farther east than Germany during his stint in the military. He also used his fists when he was angry.

I kept expecting him to tell me he knew I was fucking his wife, but once again he disappointed me when he gestured to an empty chair.

The sheriff held out a hand to Frank, who was more than happy to lean against the man's legs and have his ears rubbed.

"Someone in town called reporters about Emma," I said.

Donald nodded. "That's our guess. She's a minor, and we don't want the two of you harassed."

It was an interesting sentiment, considering the police department had looked the other way when my home and vehicle were continually vandalized in the first years following Winona and Emma's disappearance.

I looked between the men. "So you're planning a

press conference?" I asked, skepticism in my voice.

"About Winona's partial remains being found," Grover said. "We'll put a plea out to the public for information again, remind people if they find bones in the woods, they need to contact local law enforcement."

"It will give them something to write about so they can leave," the sheriff said.

"You want me to say something during the press conference," I guessed.

"A brief statement," Donald confirmed.

We spent the next few minutes going over the details that would be covered in the press conference.

Finally, Donald said, "If you want to wait in the lobby, I'll let you know when we need you. It'll be about an hour."

I stood. I knew a dismissal when I heard it, and I did not need to be reminded that I was no longer part of the boys' club.

I exited the conference room with Frank at my heels. The voices in the conference room faded behind me. The hallway was empty.

Instead of heading toward the lobby, I turned the opposite direction and moved toward my old office. The door was unlocked. I flicked the light on, ushered Frank inside, and closed the door behind us.

Everything was exactly as I had left it when I had been fired. Even the extra dog bed in the corner remained. Frank settled there now as I took a seat at the desk.

My login still worked when I powered up the computer. Footsteps rang through the hallway, and I paused, watching the door. There was no hesitation in the stride as the person in the hall passed my office. I turned back to the screen.

I brought up the portal to access the National Crime Information Center and was surprised when my credentials still permitted me entry.

I had little to go on. I did not know the girl's real name, but I could guess at her age range, height, and weight. While the system returned the results, I checked the top drawer of my desk and found a spare pair of reading glasses I had left behind.

The results for my missing person query were long. I read through the entries logged by law enforcement across the country, focusing first on the ones listed from Colorado and then on the ones listed from South Dakota. The results were both staggering and too few.

I knew the statistics. I had read the recent case study released by the Urban Indian Health Institute. The study had identified five hundred and six cases of missing and murdered American Indian and Alaska Native women and girls across seventy-one selected cities. The number was likely much higher, but there was no comprehensive data collection system regarding the number of missing and murdered women in Indian country. In 2016 alone, the NCIC had reported almost six thousand missing American Indian and Alaska Native women and girls, but the US Department of Justice's federal missing persons database only logged a little over a hundred cases.

I expanded the parameters for the date, not certain how long the kid had been on the run before she showed up in Raven's Gap. I skimmed the missing persons reports in both states for the last three months, noting the amount of women—mothers, sisters, daughters—whose cases were still open.

The climate crisis contributed to the high numbers of rape, murder, and disappearance of Native women. The oil drilling in close proximity to Indian country, or in some instances on Indian land itself, brought in vast numbers of outsiders. The outsiders were largely men. Bored, rough men far from home who were not held accountable by the law. It was a violent tragedy waiting to happen.

Quick, light steps reached me from the hall. Frank lifted his head. My office door opened before I could react, and Joan slipped inside, closing the door silently behind her.

She glanced between the computer and me. The screen was turned away from her.

"You know you can't be in here," she said softly.

I closed the browser for the NCIC portal and hit the power button on the modem as she rounded my desk. The screen went black before she could see it.

"Just looking for these." I slipped my reading glasses off and pocketed them. "I don't have an extra pair."

She shook her head as she leaned back against my desk. Frank stood and ambled to her side. She rested a slim, manicured hand on his head. "You lie well, but I know you better than that." She smiled, but there was a turmoil in her eyes I had not seen before. "Your daughter looks just like Winona."

Her words surprised me. The girl looked nothing like my wife. The only thing they shared was the dark, straight banner of hair.

She reached out and rested her palm against my cheek. Her touch surprised me as much as her words. I did not lean into her touch. I stayed still and watched her. I glanced past her to the door and cupped the curve of her hip in my hand. Her skirt was smooth and silky, catching on the calluses that roughened my fingers. I had never considered us lovers. That was too intimate a term. We shared our bodies on occasion and little more.

The sleeve of Joan's blouse slid up on her arm as she cupped the side of my face. I caught sight of the livid ring of bruises circling her forearm.

I clasped her hand in mine and drew it down between us, pushing her sleeve back to her elbow. She sucked in a breath and tried to pull away. I kept my grip light but unbreakable on her hand.

The deep purple and black bruises were shaped exactly like a hand print around her forearm. I placed my hand gently over the mark, keeping my touch light so I would not hurt her.

"Why do you stay?" I asked. I had pondered the answer to that question for ten years.

She gently extricated her hand from my grasp and pulled the sleeve of her silk blouse down to her wrist. She met my gaze evenly, and the smile that curved her lips was solemn and sad. "It's complicated."

I remembered Evelyn's words from earlier. *Isn't it always?*

Eleven

ANNIE

I opened the blinds and paused when I would have turned away. I squinted at the tree line.

It was early. The shadows were still cool and deep. Someone stood just within the shadows at the edge of the trees.

I couldn't tell if it was a man or a woman. It might be someone staying here at the inn out for a morning walk, pausing to admire the view of the river.

It was dark in my room. I hadn't turned on any lights when I got out of bed. Whoever was standing in the trees couldn't see me, I told myself.

But still I slid to the side and pressed my back against the wall. Maybe I was wrong. Maybe the person was not standing in the shadows watching the inn. Watching me.

I had been so careful. I knew they would be looking for me, and I was not certain how powerful they were. I knew they were rich enough to offer my sister something she could not resist: a chance to change her fate. I had tried to do that for her, but they had offered her more than I was able to. I knew they were resourceful enough to make her disappear until the night Charles Two Rivers from the service station showed up on my doorstep and said I had a call from her.

The moment she whispered my name, I knew this was something bigger, something dangerous. Something worth killing over.

I slid to the floor and crawled to the bed, reaching under it and dragging my backpack out. I didn't know if taking them would help at all, but I needed someone to believe me. This was all the proof I had.

I had been so careful, but I knew my face had been captured by the reporters. I had been so stupid to claim I was Emma Lewis. It had led them right to me.

I opened the backpack. All of the files I had stolen from that house outside of Denver were still there. I spread them on the floor in front of me.

I had only been able to grab what I could fit in my backpack. The walls of the room I found had been lined with file cabinets. When I broke into the house in the middle of the night, I had been looking for a single file.

I slid it from the pile now and flipped it open. *Kimimela Between Lodges* was printed neatly on the tab. The records contained nothing that told of how my sister loved to stand outside and watch storms roll over the plains. There was nothing that mentioned how infectious her laugh had been, how she had our mother's smile, how big her dreams had been. She had wanted to leave Pine Ridge, go to college, and see the world.

There was nothing in the file that told of the fear in her voice when she called me, of the desperation in her plea. She had whispered everything she knew about the organization, voice wavering and tight. She had told me names and dates, descriptions of people and places.

I placed my hand over her name.

There was nothing in the file that told of how her body had been tossed aside on the floor like a piece of trash. There was nothing written down about how this was all my fault.

I did not realize I was crying until a tear fell from my chin to the page. I brushed it away quickly, but the damage was done. The ink where she had signed her name at the bottom of the page was smeared.

The hardest thing I had ever done was to leave my sister dead on the floor in a seedy motel off Broadway in Denver. Kimi would just be a case report marked closed in their system with her race listed as "Other."

I had intended to only find her file, but when I saw the extent of the operation, I had grabbed as many as I could carry. It was all the evidence I had to prove what had happened to Kimi.

"What I did to her," I whispered.

I had failed my little sister when she was alive. I wouldn't do so now that she was gone.

I scrubbed my face free of tears and slid the files back into my backpack before tucking the bag in its hiding place.

Evelyn was in the kitchen when I entered. She sat at the small breakfast table staring out the window. Her head turned at the sound of my footsteps, and she smiled a greeting.

"I don't know what you eat for breakfast," she said, "but there is a variety of food in the pantry. Help yourself."

I settled on the easiest option: toast with jam. I took the chair opposite Evelyn. My gaze was drawn to her as I ate.

When she turned from the window and caught me staring, I flushed. "Are you and H—my dad…?"

Her lips quirked. "No, we're not."

"So you're just friends."

The quirk grew into a smile. "I'm not certain I would go that far. I moved to town in January. Your dad and I ended up helping one another, in a way."

In January, I had been at the service station and caught the headline on the old television Charles Two Rivers kept behind the counter.

"You knew Russell Jeffers?" I asked.

She flinched at the name. "I knew him as Jeff Roosevelt."

"You're the woman mentioned in the articles," I said as realization dawned. "The one who escaped and killed him."

"I haven't read any of the articles."

Her tone was polite, but I heard the abruptness in her words. Her gaze had shifted back to the window. Tension tightened her face.

The woman had been kidnapped by a serial killer and survived. Not just survived, I corrected myself. She had killed him. I could not fathom how strong and brave she was.

"I thought my mother might be one of his victims," I admitted. "As soon as I heard the news, I contacted the tribal police about sending my DNA to the FBI for comparison."

She turned back to me, the remembered horror

clearing from her face. Her brow wrinkled, and I remembered too late that I was supposed to be Emma Lewis, a little girl who had gone missing right alongside her mother. I wondered suddenly if Hector had thought the serial killer was responsible for his wife and daughter's disappearance.

Evelyn didn't question me about my identity, though. She simply asked, "Was she?"

"No." I glanced down at the crumbs on my plate. "She left home one evening ten years ago, and she never came back."

"That happens all too often to Indigenous women," she said softly.

She was right. It happened all the time in Indian country. One of my teacher's nieces had been murdered two years ago. A neighbor's daughter had gone missing six years ago. The frequency only added to the horror.

No white woman knew what our experience was like, but my hackles didn't go up at her words. I remembered her own experience.

Silence fell between us until curiosity got the better of me. "What happened to your hand?"

Evelyn didn't appear to be irritated at my nosiness. She glanced at me and then watched her hands as she flexed what fingers she did have.

She extended her hand across the table. My gaze darted to her face, and then I leaned forward and peered at the nubs of flesh where her fingers had been.

"Frostbite," she said. "I got lost in a blizzard after escaping Jeff's greenhouse. I lost part of my ear and a couple of toes, too."

I remembered a scene from a movie. "Did they just

break right off?"

Evelyn laughed. I felt my face heat. It was a stupid question, and I wished I could take it back as soon as I said it.

"No," she said, still chuckling. "At least not that I heard. Hector and Frank found me just in time. I was told the surgeons removed my fingers and toes when they realized they couldn't be saved. I don't remember any of it."

My face still felt like it was on fire, but she smiled at me.

"That would be a good story, though," she said. "I think that's the version I'll tell next time someone asks me. I snapped my fingers off when I realized they were frostbitten."

I grimaced. "I'm sorry. That was stupid."

"You don't need to apologize. That's the first time I've laughed about it."

She had left her hand on the table between us. My gaze dropped to it again.

"Does it hurt?" I ask.

She fisted her hand and then spread her fingers. "Not really, but it still feels strange to me. Parts of me are missing. I know it. I see it. But I still find myself glancing at my hand, expecting to see my fingers."

I thought about my sister. She was gone from me. I would never be reunited with her. I knew it, but I didn't feel that way. I felt like she would come through the door at any moment, smile in place, a wild story to tell me.

She had always loved to sneak up on me and scare me. Sometimes I felt a shift of air at my back, and I would turn quickly, expecting to find her behind me, expression devious and playful. At night, I rolled over and stretched a hand across the mattress, expecting to feel her warmth. But the sheets around me were cold and empty.

"You've gotten used to it, though?" I asked, tracing a finger along the edge of the table. "Parts of you gone, and you won't ever get them back?"

Pieces of me had been stripped away. First my mother, gone in the dark, taken from me by someone lurking in the dark. Then my grandmother.

I put a hand on my sister's chest. I was frozen in the doorway.

"What is it?" Kimi asked.

Something was wrong. I could feel it.

"Wait outside," I said.

She pushed at my arm blocking her entry into our home. "What's going on?"

"Just do it," I snapped at her.

Her face fell, and she turned away quickly, shoulders slumped. I wanted to go after her and tell her I was sorry, but I couldn't. I stared at the open doorway into the bedroom.

There was no rasp of breath from within. No greeting called to us as soon as the door opened. I could just see the end of the bed from where I stood, and my grandmother's feet were completely still under the quilt.

I crossed the short distance slowly, forcing one foot in front of the other until I stood in the doorway of the bedroom.

"Uncí," I whispered.

My grandmother was silent.

My breath caught in my chest, and my throat tight-

ened. I crept closer.

"Unci?" My voice shook.

She looked like she was sleeping. I touched her chest, but it remained still under my trembling hand.

One of her hands hung off the side of the bed. It was swollen and blue.

"Unci, please." I caught her hand in mine as I sank to my knees beside the bed. I pressed her cold palm against my cheek. "Unci, please. Please wake up."

I whispered it over and over again as I cried. I needed her to wake up. I needed her to stay with us.

I heard a creak of the floorboard, and then my sister burrowed against me. She clung to me, arms wrapped tightly around me.

She cried as well, but when she spoke, it was not to beg our grandmother not to leave us.

"It's okay, Annie," she whispered. "It's okay. I'm here."

And now she was gone as well.

The silence had stretched on too long, I realized. I glanced up and found Evelyn studying me.

Behind the lenses of her glasses, her eyes were almost golden in color. Like an owl's eyes, I thought. Evelyn's contained that same wise knowing I had seen in the great horned owl's that had taken up residence in the rafters of the outhouse one year.

"I wouldn't say I've gotten used to it," she said finally, voice quiet and thoughtful. "I've learned to live around the loss, and I no longer feel a sense of grief when I look at my hand and remember what's missing."

I swallowed. "Do you think that's true of…of losing someone you love, too?"

"Yes," she said immediately. "I never knew my parents. Both of them were killed the day I was born by a drunk driver."

"I'm sorry."

She nodded. "I don't know what it is to miss them, because I never had them in my life. My grandparents raised me, and I lost them both within months of one another last year. They were everything to me."

I pressed a hand to my heart. With my mother and my grandmother gone, my sister had been everything I lived for.

Evelyn's gaze dropped to my hand and then lifted to my face. "The grief was like a weight against my chest. For a long time, I thought it would crush me. For a long time, I let it crush me."

Tears pricked my eyes.

"But it's like everyone tells you." Her eyes fell to her own marred hand. "It's like this." She flexed her remaining fingers. "It takes time. Over time, you learn to live around the loss. After a while, you still feel what's missing, but the sense of grief is not so constant a companion."

It took me a moment before I could speak. "That's good to know." My voice was hoarse, my words little more than a whisper.

Twelve

HECTOR

The press conference left me with a knot of tension in my neck that no amount of rubbing would loosen. The reporters lingered around town, but none of them followed me as I pulled out of the police department parking lot.

I braked at a stop sign and stared unseeingly at the river. Instead of turning back to the inn, I took the state road and headed out of town. Frank curled up in the passenger's seat with a sigh.

It took me an hour to reach Livingston. I turned off Highway 89 and took Highway 90 thirty-five miles to Big Timber. The state highway I turned on wound back to the south through narrow valleys between rolling hills. The sun was high overhead but dulled with the haze of yellow smoke.

The road curved in the small outpost of McLeod, crossed the Boulder River, and followed the serpentine path of the river deeper into the mountains. The rough blacktop eventually ran out a few miles from my destination.

There was not much to Contact, Montana. It was not even a widening in the road. There had been a post office here once, back in the gold mining days, but it had been shut down in 1935. The East Boulder Mine in the mountains to the west was still operational, though it sourced palladium and platinum, not gold.

I was not certain if some of the miners lived in Contact. After the gold mines ceased production, it was a place one retreated to in order to escape civilization. Or to hide a pair of bodies.

I did not know who in this place that could not quite be called a town had found Winona's skull. I did know that if I went knocking on doors, I would likely be met with a shotgun blast to the chest.

There was a campground south of the short, sparse sprawl of Contact. I pulled off the road and parked in an empty campground lot.

Frank bounded out of the cab after me. I grabbed my rifle from the hooks in the back window.

The brass frame of the Henry Lever Action .45-70 had a rich patina from years of use, and I preferred the octagon barrel over the round. I removed the tubular magazine, ensured the chamber was empty, and closed the lever. I thumbed the hammer down and dropped four rounds into the magazine before I inserted the tube and cycled the action to chamber a round. I reached into the box I kept under my seat and pocketed eight more rounds of ammo.

The Henry was a classic rifle. The .45-70 kicked like a son of a bitch and packed a mother of a one-shot drop on most game. I had never had the opportunity to test it, and hoped I never would, but I thought it would at least slow a grizzly's charge. I carried it over my shoulder and whistled for Frank as I set off into the woods. He followed at my heels as I cut through the trees to the river.

The mountains were steep and rugged here, hemming in the valley from the east and the west. The wilderness was only a few steps from the rough gravel road.

Frank forded into the shallows of the water. I picked my way across the river, Frank splashing at my side. The water was cold but shallow, no deeper than my knees at its widest in this spot.

Contact might be only a hundred yards behind me, but already the wilds had forgotten a near-abandoned outpost of humanity existed on the other side of the water.

We headed northwest into the mountains, skirting the valley of a scree field that would be prime avalanche territory in winter. There was no trail to follow, except the one of our own making. Frank stayed at my side, gaze and nose keen and alert.

I looked for the white wolf, but she had proven herself to be flesh and blood, not a harbinger of a descent into insanity. A wolf had its territory, and she did not appear to guide me in my search for what remained of Winona and Emma.

I hated to think of them as *remains*. It was a word I had no problem using for the men, women, and children Frank and I had searched for but had not known. The term did not make me flinch when I had written or read it in police reports.

But my girls were more than bones stripped bare by

time, exposure, and animals. *Remains* said nothing of the gift Winona had with horses, the fierce loyalty she felt for those she loved, the deep well of kindness and generosity she contained, the way her arms had always been open to me. *Remains* did not give testament to my daughter's love of animals, the wonder in her expression the first time she had seen snow, how she looked at everything with bright curiosity, the way she would laugh and clap her hands every time my wife would sing to her of a little Lakota girl with green eyes who ran with wolves and danced on the wind.

Even the skull sitting on the table beside my bed at the inn held nothing of what had made my wife the woman she was. There was nothing left of them in the bones. Even so, I wanted those bones brought home to me.

Frank and I reached the crest of the ridge. I took a deep breath, and it tasted of wildfire smoke. For the moment, there was no wind. Beneath the acrid odor of smoke, the air was thick with the smell of spruce and pine heated by the summer temperatures. The sun was warm on my head and against the back of my neck.

Our climb had not given me much of a vantage point. The trees were too thick. The angle of the climb was steep, but the pinnacle was not exposed rock face.

I rubbed my chest. My heart knocked hard against my palm. I was breathing harder than I normally would be. For a moment, the feeling of being trapped swept over me, as sudden and violent as a wave. The trees felt as if they were closing in on me, the mountains around me growing tall enough to block out the sky.

I closed my eyes and struggled to draw in a deep

breath, but all I could do was pant shallowly. The last fifteen years was a growing knot in my chest and throat.

Frank whined and leaned against my legs. I did not give him the signal to search. I had no idea where to even begin. I had simply needed to come breathe the air here in the mountains where that small piece of her had been found, where she and Emma possibly still remained. And now I could not seem to draw a full breath.

It was the *possibly* that had always been in question. The uncertainty, the not knowing, the lack of fucking answers. The wilderness was like the tide, always carrying bones far from where they lay. My girls could be right under my feet, only a few shovels of dirt away, or they could be fifty, a hundred miles deeper into the wilderness.

The knot in my chest erupted, hot like lava, turbulent like the sea.

"*Winona!*" I shouted her name, and Frank startled beside me. Birds took flight with an unsettled shriek. "*Emma!*"

Frank began to bark, lending his voice to mine as I shouted their names over and over again.

The mountains trembled with the sound, echoing my calls. I shouted as loudly as I could. I cupped my hands around my mouth and turned in all directions screaming for them. My face was hot. My heart surged so hard I thought I might have a heart attack.

Nothing but the echo responded.

I shouted until my voice was a hoarse croak, until my calls were no more than a whisper.

I stumbled. A fine tremor moved through me, and it felt like it had the force of an earthquake.

Frank fell silent when I did. The poodle panted. He was alert and agitated, glancing all around us.

A tremor went through him as well when I laid a hand on his head. I wanted to reassure him, but my throat was too raw to form words.

Instead, once my legs were steady under me, I started down the mountain. Frank loped ahead of me, leading the way back to the river.

I stooped when we reached the water. It ran clear and pure over the rocks, and I drank from my cupped palms. The coolness eased some of the discomfort in my throat and chased away some of the heat from my skin when I splashed handfuls over my head. Frank lapped at the water beside me, and he leaned into my hand when I rested it on his side.

My truck was where I had left it in the empty campground. I rolled the windows down on the two-hour drive back to Raven's Gap, letting the smoky wind whip through the cab to clear away the remnants of the trembling heat that had swept over me.

My hands had stopped shaking and my heart had slowed by the time I reached town. The sun was sinking in the west, halfway into its descent into the horizon.

I did not see any reporters still parked around town, but the man standing on the sidewalk in front of the inn grabbed my attention. I slowed to a halt and watched him.

He turned at the sound of my truck. He was a stranger, not a local. This was a dead end residential street, where the only business was the inn. I did not think he was looking for a room for the night.

"You lost?" My voice was even more hoarse than usual.

"Nope," he responded. "Just stretching my legs and taking in the sights."

He pivoted and strolled casually down the sidewalk as if to prove his point. I let my truck idle in the middle of the street. I watched him in the rearview mirror until a dark vehicle pulled up to the curb at the end of the street and he slipped inside. It was too far away for me to see the tags.

I parked in front of the inn, and once inside, Frank went to his water bowl in the kitchen as I went to the cabinet for a glass. The water from the sink's tap was cold against my raw throat.

The hum of a drill reached me. After I drank another glass of water, I followed the sound through the inn to the back deck. I stopped in the doorway.

The girl must have seen movement out of the corner of her eye. She released the trigger on the drill and turned.

I glanced around, taking in the neat line of shutters leaning against the deck.

She set the drill aside and clasped her hands nervously. "I found your tools. I hope that's okay."

I moved closer to inspect her work. The board and batten shutters were neatly made, the spacing even and straight, the handiwork sturdy.

When I said nothing, she continued, "I watched a tutorial on how to make them on YouTube. I…" She swallowed. "I messed up on the first two. I'm sorry.

But I think the rest turned out really well. I used some wood glue I found before I used the screws."

I rubbed a finger over the head of the screw embedded in the wood. "If you put your screws in from the bottom, it doesn't show the hardware."

Her brow wrinkled as she studied the shutters she had made. Her shoulders slumped, and her face fell.

"Just telling you for future reference," I said, the words scraping over my throat. "These are good. You did a great job."

The light came back on in her eyes. "You really think so?"

"Yep. Saved me a day's worth of work and did a better job than I could. I never get the spacing right." I said the lie easily just to see her shoulders straighten and the look of pride in her face.

"I used nails to make sure I got the spacing even," she said, "and Evelyn let me borrow her phone and use the level."

I ran a hand over the shutter on the sawhorse, studying how she had used clamps, how the measurements on the boards were marked neatly in pencil. "Very nice craftsmanship."

The kid practically beamed, and the brightness of that smile reminded me of Winona's when I first met her.

"You want to help me mount these on the windows tomorrow?"

She nodded. "You're not getting sick, are you?"

"No," I said hoarsely.

"Betty called earlier to check on me," she said. "Can I go over to their house for supper? I just want to make sure they're okay. I'm sure you can come, too."

I had not seen any vans with news station logos on them as I had come through town. "Go on," I said. "I'll clean up here. Just call and let me know if you're coming back here tonight or staying with them." The words were out before I could call them back, and I was surprised to hear how fatherly they sounded.

"I will," she promised, voice earnest.

She scooped her backpack up from a chair on the deck and darted inside. Frank started to follow her, but I called him back to me. He settled on the deck with a sigh as I moved to inspect the rest of the shutters she had made.

I was impressed. The kid was a good hand with tools.

I heard the front door of the inn slam as I started to put away the tools she had used. The faint sound of an engine cranking brought my head up.

I almost went back to work, but unease nipped at me. The man standing on the front walk of the inn loomed in my mind.

"Frank," I called.

The poodle's head lifted from his paws. He stood and stretched and then loped to my side. He trotted at my heels as I moved through the inn and jogged up the drive to the street.

The same dark sedan I had seen earlier was at the end of the street. I watched the vehicle creep slowly down the lane and turn back to the right. The tag on the vehicle was a California plate, and I committed the license to memory.

I glanced into the forest across the street. I could

no longer see the girl. The woods, thick with summer growth, had swallowed her. The unfamiliar car was heading the same direction she was.

That same sense of unease prompted me to cross the street. Frank's nose went up, and I knew he had caught the girl's scent trail when he paced back and forth for a moment before darting ahead of me and breaking the tree line.

I followed him. The stretch of woods between was narrow, no wider than fifty yards, with houses tucked back into the trees. The forest thinned until it deposited me on the next street. I glanced around, wondering if the girl had continued into the woods across the road or if she had taken the sidewalk into town.

Frank paced along the street, nose working. I waited, watching him. He would let me know which way the girl had gone.

I turned, searching the sidewalk, and spotted the dark vehicle parked at the end of the street. The windows were so deeply tinted I could not tell if anyone was inside the car, but one of the doors was ajar.

I started toward it.

Frank growled suddenly.

I turned back to him. "What is it, boy?"

His lips were curled back in a snarl, and a low rumble rolled through his chest. He bolted into the forest just as a terrified scream ripped through the air.

Thirteen

ANNIE

A vehicle was parked along the street. It was dark and nondescript, the windows so heavily tinted I could not see inside.

I hesitated before stepping off the curb, remembering the vehicle that had attempted to run me over. That had not been an accident.

The engine did not rev as I crossed the street. It didn't even move when I cut into the woods.

I glanced over my shoulder several times, weaving through the trees. No one followed me, and the car stayed parked the entire time I was able to keep it in my sight.

The trees felt like they gathered protectively around me. I liked the feeling. At home, with the plains like a golden ocean, it felt like my community existed on a small island, exposed to the elements.

In summer months, the wind sang. In the winter, it screamed. It hurled itself unrelentingly against anything that dared to stand in its way. The wind on the plains was as finely honed as a blade, cutting right through flesh down to the bone. The wind scraped the land raw.

Not many trees could maintain their vigil against such harassment, but I found I liked how it felt like they were guarding, protecting, and guiding me as I wound my way through the woods.

When I stepped from their embrace and crossed the street, movement at the end of the lane caught my eye. I froze.

The dark, nondescript vehicle that had been parked down the street from the inn drove slowly down the road. It paused, the brakes soundless, when whoever was hidden within the blackened glass caught sight of me.

The car's occupants had been looking for me, I realized. They had cut a parallel path on the street to what I had taken through the woods. I tried to tell myself that it was probably just a reporter who had stayed in town hoping for more of a story to tell.

The vehicle didn't turn. It just idled in the road, waiting to see which way I would go. I wanted to be brave and walk right up to the car with a rock in hand and break out the glass. I had my backpack on, though. All the evidence I had was in the bag. If they took it, I would have nothing. They would disappear, and I would fail my sister again.

I remembered her sightless eyes and the ring of bruises around her throat.

I ran.

I darted into the woods. My feet always had wings, but I couldn't spread those wings like I usually did with the trees around me. What had felt protective moments ago now felt caging. Branches reached out and tried to grab me, slowing my race deeper into the forest.

I leapt over fallen logs and shoved through the underbrush. Running was all about breathing, but I couldn't seem to get enough air into my lungs. The push and pull of breath was rough and winded.

I looked back and tripped over a root. I hit the ground hard, driving the air from my lungs. My chin bounced against the dirt, and I felt the already wounded hide of my palms and knees tear again. Stars spiraled across my vision. I lay there, stunned, the blood rushing in my ears.

The snap of a twig underfoot brought my head up, but I was too slow to react. A hard jerk on my backpack yanked me to my knees.

"No!" I cried. I held on to the straps as tightly as I could.

I caught glimpses of the man as I struggled to get away. He was white and dressed in black with a ball cap pulled low over his brow.

His hand fisted in the looped handle of my backpack. My hair had fallen loose from its braid, and strands were tangled with his fingers. His hard, rough attempts to drag the backpack off my shoulders ripped my hair at the roots. The tearing in my scalp burned like he held a flame to my skin.

I screamed, as loudly as I could, fear and pain and anger lending strength to my voice. At the same time, I stopped wrestling against the man and threw myself back against his legs.

He staggered, and his grip loosened. I lunged forward, breaking his grip, and snatched up a fallen limb that was as long and thick as my arm.

I swung it as I spun, gripping it like a baseball bat. He was taller than I realized, though, and my makeshift weapon cracked across his shoulder instead of the side of his head. He stumbled with the blow, but he didn't fall. I swung again. His hand shot out and caught the end of the limb before it could make contact.

"Fuck this," he snapped, voice as hard as his eyes.

He yanked my weapon away from me. It was my turn to stagger as the limb tore from my grip, scraping my raw palms. He tossed the limb aside. Before I could recover, the back of his hand cracked across my face.

I fell. My ears rang from the blow, and my cheek turned hot, throbbing with my racing heartbeat.

"Jesus, Dave," another voice said. I hadn't realized two men had followed me into the woods. "She said to just get the files and not hurt the kid."

"Did you see her just try to bash my brains out?" the man who had grabbed me snapped. He took a menacing step toward me. I tried to hide my flinch. "Just give me the backpack."

I held on to the straps with all of my strength and kicked at him.

"Fine," he said. "We'll do this the hard way."

"Ah, hell," the other man sighed. My gaze swung to him, but he made no move to help me.

A white streak darted through the woods. For a moment, I thought it was the white wolf I had seen last night.

"What the—?" The other man stumbled back.

Frank raced past him. The man who stood over me turned at his friend's outcry. He didn't have time to brace himself. When the poodle leapt at him and sank those sharp canine teeth into the man's arm, he screamed as he was knocked to the ground.

I scrambled away. The man struggled against Frank's grip on his arm, but the dog's jaws were clenched tightly in his flesh. Blood splattered on the ground. Frank's snarls could be heard even over the man's shrieks.

The man writhed on the ground. He swung at Frank twice before his hand scrabbled in the dirt. When I saw his fingers close over a large rock, I lunged forward.

"No!" I shouted.

Before he even had a chance to lift the rock for a blow, a boot connected with the side of his head. He went limp immediately. The rock fell from his grasp.

I looked up at Hector. He was staring at the other man. I followed his gaze and sucked in a breath when I saw the gun in the other man's hands.

"I suggest you get your friend and get the fuck out of here," Hector said. His voice was hard and cold.

The man took a careful step toward us, his gun fixed on Hector. "We don't want any trouble," he said. "We just want what's in the backpack."

Hector didn't lift his hands. He didn't even seem to notice the gun pointed right at him. "You started trouble the moment you followed her. I won't give you a second chance."

I crawled closer until I was behind Hector. I stayed huddled on the ground. My legs weren't ready to work yet.

Whatever the other man saw in Hector's face, it made him tuck his gun away.

Hector took a step back as the man approached.

"Frank," he said. "Leave it."

The poodle was panting. His muzzle was stained with blood. He obeyed, and the man's shredded arm flopped into the dirt. Frank trotted to my side.

This time, I felt no leeriness at his approach. When he reached me, I wrapped an arm around him. He leaned against me. We both trembled.

The man said nothing more. He hauled his bloody friend over his shoulder and disappeared into the woods, never looking back.

Once the man was out of sight, Hector's gaze fell to me. I realized that I held on to his dog with one hand and clung to the hem of his jeans with the other. His jaw tightened as he stared at me.

"Drugs or cash?" he asked.

I blinked up at him. "What?" I whispered, still reeling from what had happened.

"In your backpack," he said. "Drugs or cash?"

I shook my head. "Neither. It's not like that."

"They'll be back."

I couldn't tell if it was a question or a statement, but I nodded.

I sucked in an uneven breath and felt my chin begin to tremble. My face felt tender and bruised, my scalp burned, and I couldn't stop shaking.

"I thought you said Frank was a search and rescue dog," I said. I could hear the quaver in my voice.

Hector knelt, and I relinquished my grip on his pant leg. He ran his hands over Frank's neck and sides. The poodle leaned into his touch. I was surprised to see how gentle Hector was with him.

"Frank has a number of talents," he said.

He turned to me, and for a moment, I caught sight of the ease in the hard coldness of his face. It wasn't a gentleness, and it wasn't a softness in his expression. I didn't think he had either in him. But he clearly cared about his dog, and for a brief instant, that expression was directed at me.

Even though the hardness settled back over his face, he extended his hand to me. "You need some ice for that bruise."

I let him help me to my feet. My knees felt like water when I stood, though. Before I could sink back to the ground, Hector lifted me in his arms.

He carried me through the woods. Frank trotted at his heels. I closed my eyes and rested my head against his shoulder. I wanted to pretend just for a moment that he was really my dad and that he really cared.

Fourteen

HECTOR

Maggie exited the kitchen as I closed her office door behind me. She paused when she caught sight of me.

"Wait here a moment while I deliver these plates?"

I nodded and moved after her down the hall until I had a clear view into the diner. The girl sat at a table away from the wide windows. Ed and Betty sat with her, and Betty's arm was wrapped tightly around the girl's shoulders.

The girl held a pack of frozen peas to her bruised cheek. Her hair was piled on top of her head, revealing the raw strip of flesh at the nape of her neck where her hair had been torn from her scalp. Maggie had slicked ointment over the area but had not bandaged it for fear of the adhesive tape pulling out more of her hair.

Ed glanced over the women's shoulders and nodded at me.

Maggie came around the corner, her hands empty. She caught my arm, and I let her lead me back to her office.

"I called Jack," I said. "Ed and Betty will want her to

go home with them, but those men who grabbed her in the woods will be back. If not them, others. If she's not with me, I want their house being watched. I want someone there protecting her. He said he'd stay with them tonight."

"Good," Maggie said. She closed the door to her office behind us.

Frank and Louie lifted their heads and then resumed their nap on Maggie's couch. I had washed the blood from Frank's muzzle while Maggie took care of the girl.

"Are you alright?" she asked.

"Why wouldn't I be?"

She sent me an arched look as she leaned against her desk. "Because I can practically hear your teeth grinding all the way over here."

"The kid has been lying to me from the moment she set foot in town."

"Did it ever occur to you that she lied about being Emma to get you to listen to her in the first place?" Maggie said quietly.

I remembered the way I had dismissed her each time I encountered her until she had claimed to be my daughter.

"That doesn't tell me how she knew about Emma to begin with," I said. "The kid obviously did her research. I just don't know what she's looking for here."

"Why don't you ask her? She came here for you specifically. She sought you out."

"If she wanted money, she would have tried to steal it already." I paced back and forth. Adrenalin still coursed through me, and I could not quell the rush of tension it had sent flooding through my system.

"You're not blind," Maggie said. "Surely you've seen how she looks to you for approval, how she soaks up the attention from Ed and Betty. She's not here for money."

"Whatever brought her here, that kid is keeping secrets that are dangerous." I turned away from her discerning gaze and rubbed the back of my neck. "They're going to get her hurt." I blew out a breath. "They *did* get her hurt."

"You protected her," Maggie said. "You—"

"I'm not her father," I snapped. "It's not my fucking responsibility to protect her."

The words were out before I could call them back. They rang in the air between us. Maggie stared at me, eyes wide. Both dogs sat up at my tone. Frank whined, his tail thumping uncertainly on the cushion.

I met Maggie's gaze, jaw tight. I did not understand why a tremor still rattled through me. It had begun as soon as I heard the girl scream. My heart thumped in my chest, its pace suggesting I was still running like I had been the moment I heard her cry.

I had not been close enough to do anything when I saw the man strike her, the force so hard it knocked her to the ground. All I could do was send Frank ahead of me to protect her. When I kicked the man in the head, it had taken everything in me not to keep kicking until his head was caved in and his brain was splattered on my boot.

I did not want this tumult of emotion that made me feel so unsteady and uncertain.

As Maggie and I stared at one another, I watched the shock fade from her face and a hard mask fall over her features. It was a look I had never seen on her before.

"I love you, Hector," Maggie said, voice hard. "But you're a fucking idiot."

I blinked. She had always been honest with me, but she had never been harsh. Her eyes were cold as she met my gaze now, though, and her lips were pressed into a thin line.

"Winona was pregnant when she disappeared," she said.

The words were a blow. I staggered when they hit me. I moved carefully to the couch and sat down before my legs gave out.

"I was the only person she told. She hadn't even been to the doctor yet. I didn't tell anyone after she and Emma went missing, because it just would have added to the grief. And..." She hesitated. "It would have made even more suspicion fall on you."

She was not wrong. Everyone in town knew of my apathy for my daughter and my wife. I could imagine the suspicion I would have faced had it been known that Winona was pregnant at the time of her disappearance.

I had never been interested in being a father. People would have thought that learning I was going to be so a second time was the last straw. They would have thought that when she told me she was pregnant, I had snapped. They would have accused me of killing her, killing Emma, to escape fatherhood, a role I had never wanted.

"She was afraid to tell you," Maggie said. "Do you know why?" Even if I had an answer for her, she did not pause long enough for me to respond. "Because she knew you had no interest in being a father. She knew you viewed her and Emma as a burden. She knew you would feel the same way about another baby." I closed my eyes, but she kept speaking. "She knew you were a cold, unfeeling bastard, and while that might have dampened her joy, it never poisoned her love for you. It exhausted her love, but it never destroyed it."

Heavy silence fell between us.

I did not hear her move until I felt the couch dip beside me. She sat beside me, still and quiet, for several long minutes.

Her fingers landed on my wrist. I opened my eyes and stared down at her hand. Her skin was dark against mine, her fingers strong and callused. She squeezed my wrist and then her hand slid down to grasp mine. I remained still as she leaned against my side and rested her head on my shoulder.

"I'm sorry," she whispered. "That was wrong of me. You're not cold and unfeeling. I should never have said that."

Frank shifted on the couch on my opposite side until he was able to rest his head on my knee.

Maggie squeezed my hand and then reached over and combed her fingers through Frank's topknot. "I don't know your story, Hector. I don't know why you're afraid to love someone. I don't know why you're afraid to let someone love you in return."

I said nothing. I was not afraid. It had never been about fear. It was about ability. I had no love inside of me to give.

When the silence had stretched between us for minutes again, Maggie said softly, "I'm not asking you to play dad. I'm asking you to please not turn your back on the child sitting out in the diner."

The anger and fear that had burgeoned inside of me as soon as I heard the girl scream were going to suffocate me.

"It's not my place to ask," Maggie said, "I realize that. And it's not because she needs you, though she clearly does. I'm asking you because *you* need *her*."

Fifteen

ANNIE

I curled up on the neatly made bed and clutched the raggedy stuffed rabbit to my chest. My cheek pulsed with my heartbeat.

Hector had left the diner with his face even more of a cold, hard mask than usual. Frank had trotted at his side to keep up with Hector's quick steps.

He was a stranger to me, and I was nothing but a false burden to him. But still I had stumbled to my feet and rushed across the diner. I shoved through the door and stood on the sidewalk. He held the door of his truck open long enough for Frank to leap in. He slammed the door, and then the engine roared to life. He pulled out of the diner's lot with a squeal of tires.

He never once glanced back at me.

And why should he? My breath was caught in my throat right alongside my heart. He had every reason to hate me. I was lying about being the daughter he must have loved. I had caused him nothing but trouble, and now this. His dog could have been hurt by those men. He could have been shot.

It was all my fault.

But he hadn't even glanced back. The overwhelming urge to run after him, calling for him to not leave me behind, made me tremble where I stood.

Everyone left me, whether they wanted to or not. Everyone left, and I was always the one standing alone watching them disappear into the distance. My mother, my grandmother, my sister.

My breath hitched harder in my throat, tight and aching. My eyes burned.

"I hurt him."

I jumped. I hadn't heard the door open behind me. Maggie moved to stand at my side. When I glanced at her, I found her staring at the spot Hector's truck had disappeared from. Her face was tight with remorse.

She met my gaze, and my heart lurched at the sadness in her eyes.

"This has nothing to do with you," she said, seeming to read my face as much as I read hers. "I said things I shouldn't have. Told him something he didn't know, and then I was cruel."

"Why?" I couldn't help but ask. I felt anger rising up in me, and I realized it was directed at her.

Hector was her friend. Friends didn't deliberately hurt one another.

Her lips twisted, and she looked away. "Because for a long time, I've wanted him to care about something other than vengeance. I've wanted him to know—" She stopped herself, biting off the rest of what she was going to say. "It doesn't matter why. It just matters that I did," she said softly.

Hector might be a jerk, but from what I'd seen of

him, he had never hurt someone. He was abrupt and rude, but not mean. Just because someone was a jerk didn't mean they should be hurt.

"That wasn't cool, Maggie," I said, defensiveness slipping into my voice.

"You're right," she agreed. "It wasn't."

Ed and Betty took me home with them. Now, I listened to the quiet murmur of their voices downstairs. I had told them I was tired. It was true, but I couldn't sleep. I had tucked my backpack deep under the recesses of the bed.

I hugged the stuffed animal tight to my chest. I couldn't stay here. I couldn't let Ed and Betty or even Hector be hurt. I thought I needed someone like Hector to help me. Maybe I was just afraid to do this myself and wanted to depend on someone else.

I had always done things myself. When my mother disappeared, I had been six years old. My grandmother was actually my great-grandmother. She had been old and ill, and though she had cared for us, I knew it was my responsibility to raise my little sister with my mother gone. Kimi had been two at the time.

My grandmother had died when I was eleven. There had been no one after that to claim us. I was terrified they would take Kimi away from me, that they would take us away from the only home we had ever known.

So I lied. I closed up the one bedroom in our house, the bedroom where my grandmother had died in her bed. When people asked how she was, I told them she wasn't feeling well and wasn't up to leaving the house, but she was in good spirits.

That summer was the worst of my life as the smell of

death and rotting permeated the house. I burned sage, but it still felt like the smell clung to everything. I still gagged at the memory. Now, that smell was intertwined in my mind with fear. Because I had been so afraid someone would show up and it would all be over. I had hidden my grandmother's death, so they would think I had killed her. They would throw me in jail, and Kimi would be alone. She would have no one to take care of her, no one to look after her, no one to help her dream of something different.

The smell had finally died, but I never opened that locked bedroom door. The fear didn't die, though. It had remained. It had festered and rotted just like my grandmother's body. I was certain people could smell my fear, and I was certain it smelled exactly like my grandmother as she wasted away.

A creak of movement on the stairs brought my head up, but the footsteps did not come toward my door. They moved slowly down the hall. I heard the door to Betty and Ed's room open and close quietly.

My great-grandmother's arms had always been open to me. It was what I missed most once she was gone. When my sister turned ten, it was like a switch was thrown. Gone was the sweet, cuddly little girl I had raised. In her place was a pre-teen who was prickly and defiant and thought I was dumber than dirt. She rolled her eyes at everything I said and shoved off my hugs.

At night, once she had fallen asleep, I crept closer to her on our shared mattress until my back was pressed against hers. She gave off heat like a furnace, but even in the sweltering temperatures of summer, I savored that stolen physical contact.

I left the stuffed rabbit against the pillow and crept from my room. I thought it was Betty I had heard climbing the stairs. I paused outside her bedroom door. I told myself I was being ridiculous, but my hand still knocked tentatively on the door.

"Come in," she called.

I cracked the door and peered inside. Betty sat in bed propped up against a stack of pillows. The tv on the dresser was set to a low hum of noise.

The vast amount of medicine on her nightstand reminded me of her illness, and my throat tightened.

"Could I...Would you mind if I hung out with you?" I asked tentatively.

"I would love your company." She patted the space beside her. I crossed the room and crawled into bed. When I hesitated, Betty smiled at me. "It's alright."

Unable to resist, I curled on my side and rested my head on her leg. It felt thin and fragile beneath my cheek, and it made me worry I was leaning too heavily against her.

Her hand came to rest on my head. When she began to comb my hair with her fingers, my eyes slid shut. I squeezed them together tightly to keep the burning in my eyes contained.

Hector's voice on the television grabbed my attention, though. I opened my eyes to see a replay of the press conference in front of the police department. He spoke in that gruff, abrupt way he had, and he was only a tightening of his mouth away from scowling at the reporters.

Betty's fingers paused in my hair as he spoke about his wife and daughter. I reached back and caught her hand in mine, pulling it around me until I tucked our clasped hands under my chin.

Somewhere offscreen, someone called to Hector, "Is it true your daughter has been returned after all these years?"

I held my breath, waiting for his answer.

He was silent for a long moment. Then he said, "That's correct."

Questions erupted from the reporters clustered around, but he turned around and walked away.

Someone in uniform stepped forward and spoke about giving the family privacy during this time.

The news rolled on. Betty and I sat in silence as the screen flicked blue light around the room.

"Have you ever made a mistake you really wish you could undo?" I asked finally, voice barely a whisper.

I wasn't certain if she had heard me or if she wasn't going to answer, she was quiet for so long. Finally, her free hand came up to rest on my head. "We never gave him a chance."

"Who?"

"Hector." She sighed. "When you're an old woman like me, you'll start to think back on your life. The good things, and the bad. And you'll see more clearly where you were wrong." She was silent for a few moments, and I didn't want to interrupt her. "We were unfair to him, from the very beginning. We didn't see what Winona saw in him. I didn't see it. Not at first. All I saw was the hardness in him."

"What did she see?"

She didn't answer me immediately. I tipped my head back and peered at her face, but her gaze was on the television. I didn't think she saw what was on the screen. "That he was lost," she said finally. "And that he always had been."

I turned my face back to the TV and thought about the man who had been on the screen moments ago. I didn't see what Winona saw, either. I saw a man who looked like he never smiled.

"Ed and Jack were convinced he killed Winona and Emma," she said. "I never tried to sway them. Men need something to cling to when they feel helpless, and sometimes hate is as good as anything. But I knew he hadn't killed them."

"How did you know?" I asked.

She made a soft, noncommittal noise but otherwise remained silent.

I thought about how I had known my sister was dead even before I found her. How I had awakened in the middle of the night after her phone call. I had startled awake, unable to breathe. My throat felt constricted, my air cut off. I had staggered outside and fallen to my hands and knees, eyes streaming. When the phantom pressure around my throat suddenly loosened, I sucked in a sobbing breath, choking and gasping.

When the tears stopped streaming from my eyes and when the ache in my throat was gone, I had grabbed what I needed and stuffed it in a backpack. I had stolen Charles Two Rivers's car. I drove as quickly as I could without risking being pulled over by the cops.

But the entire drive to Denver, I had known what I would find. I was not surprised to see the bruises around my sister's throat when I found her sprawled on the dirty motel room floor.

"I—" My voice caught in my throat. "I'm not—"

Maggie had told me they knew, but I couldn't form the words. I imagined Betty and Ed casting me out of their warm, beautiful home, disappointment and hate replacing the kindness in their eyes. I remembered Hector's coldness and disinterest when I had just been some kid he couldn't be bothered to speak to.

My lips refused to shape the words I needed to say.

"You're not Emma," Betty said.

My breath stuttered. I held myself completely still, not even daring to blink.

"You're not Emma," she repeated, voice soft. "But I like to think that if she had lived, she would be as strong and courageous as you."

I didn't realize I was crying until the blanket under my cheek began to feel damp.

She gently disengaged her hand from mine. Instead of pushing me away, though, I felt her fingers begin to work the long strands of my hair into a braid.

"My sister was murdered," I whispered. "Someone killed her and left her on the floor of a dirty motel room in Denver. Like she was a…a piece of trash." I sucked in a shuddering breath. "And it's all my fault."

"No," Betty said. "Whatever happened, you're not responsible."

"I am." The dampness in the blanket beneath my cheek spread. "And I thought Hector was the only one who could help me give her some small amount of justice." I swallowed. "That's why I came here. And why I…I lied. I—"

The phone on the other bedside table suddenly began to ring. I jumped at the sudden jangle of noise.

"Can you grab that?" Betty asked.

"I've got it," I assured her. I crawled across the wide bed and grabbed the receiver. "Hello?" There was only silence, and I pressed the phone closer to my ear. "Hello?"

"Did you really think you could get away with it?" a voice asked on the other end of the line.

I froze. The blood drained from my head. I placed a hand against the headboard to steady myself.

"I want what is mine, Annie," she said softly. "I'll see you soon."

A click signaled she had ended the call.

My ear hurt from how tightly I had the phone pressed against it, and my fingers cramped with how hard I gripped the phone. My hand shook as I replaced the phone in the receiver.

"Who was it?" Betty asked.

"N-no one," I lied. "Just a wrong number."

Sixteen

HECTOR

I was born in a bathroom stall at a truck stop somewhere off Interstate 80 in Nebraska. I did not know where exactly. I did not know how old my mother was at the time, but as an adult looking back, I thought she must have been around fifteen or sixteen. I did not know who my father was or even the exact day I was born.

I had vague memories of sleeping on the floorboard of the backseat of the car we lived in. Fleeting impressions of being small and afraid and cold, curled between the seats, waiting for my mother to return from staying the night with strange men in a motel room.

It was a pattern through the first years of my life. Living in a car; sometimes sleeping on the dirty, stained floor of a motel room closet after my mother finished servicing whichever new man had bought her time and feigned interest for the night; other times I thought we had stayed in abandoned homes or buildings that smelled of shit and decay, where rats crept under the threadbare towel I used for a blanket and nipped at my fingertips.

My first clear memory was of cleaning up my mother's vomit when she had returned from a bender. I thought I was around four at the time. If I dug deeper into that memory, I could also recall her slurred words as she lay on the floor watching me.

"I hate you," she whispered. "I wish you'd never been born."

There were other words I remembered her saying. *You ruined my life. I should have drowned you in the toilet after I had you.*

When I was a boy, I had wondered if there was truth to my mother's words. If there were some people who should never have been born. If because of that, things like home and happiness were denied them. If those people who should never have been born were always on the outside of life looking in, able to see what others had but never able to achieve it for themselves.

Sometimes I still wondered that. Even more so now with Maggie's words still ringing in my head.

Frank whined at my side as I detoured from the state road and followed the rough path I had worn into a lane over the last thirty years. I had purchased fifty acres of land in the rugged northern reaches of the Black Canyon of the Yellowstone when Winona and I first moved here from Cody, Wyoming.

There was little hint of what had transpired three months ago over the course of the two-mile drive to the meadow where I had parked the Airstream. The yellow caution tape that had been tied between two trees at the end of the drive was gone, though the clearing still looked as if a bomb had been detonated in it. Trees were snapped and splintered.

When Grant Larson's men had ambushed me, setting my trailer ablaze and shooting my dog, I had blasted my way out courtesy of the dynamite William Silva, Maggie's son and a former FBI agent, had purchased for me on one of his trips to South America. I had always expected a war to come to my doorstep, and I had been prepared.

It was dark. I killed the engine and cut the lights. Frank leapt out of the cab when I opened the door and ran off into the darkness to explore his old territory. I had swung by the inn, because I needed to bring what was left of her with me. I collected the box and sat on the lowered tailgate, waiting for my eyes to adjust to the night.

The meadow had been scorched earth and destruction three months ago, but nature had proved once again that it could heal its wounds. The only thing that marred the meadow now was the burned, warped carcass of my home.

It had been little more than a tin can, but I had bought it in place of a ring for Winona. I was seventeen when Jed died, and I had no desire to spend my years toiling in backbreaking labor. That first time at the Cheyenne Frontier Days, I did not have a leather riding glove and had not known I needed one until my hand was scored and shredded after that first ride. I watched the bull I was slated, a cantankerous bastard named Nero, paying attention to the way he spun to the right as soon as he left the chute.

When it was my turn, I held on to the rope like my life depended on it, kept my hips square and my weight down, and squeezed Nero's sides with my thighs and knees. When the crossbred Charbray flew out of the gate, it felt as if I had been thrown from the top of a skyscraper with a fifteen-hundred-pound weight tied to my arm. It was all light and sound and a down-force that felt as if it were going to yank my arm out of socket.

The eight seconds felt as if they crept by at the pace of centuries, and when the buzzer finally screeched, I hit the dirt with a broken thumb, a score of eighty, and, in the end, thirty-five hundred dollars in cash.

I applied for membership with the Professional Rodeo Cowboys Association. I kept riding, and I kept winning. Within a few years, I was able to apply for membership to the Professional Bull Riders. I raked in the buckles and the prizes, but I was still sleeping in my truck seven years later when I met Winona.

She was a barrel racer, and the dark banner of her hair, the wide, white gleam of her smile, and the bounce of her tits caught my eye the first time I saw her in the saddle. I did not know anything about love, but I knew about lust. In the ensuing year, I never tired of fucking her, and when she had begun to talk about marriage, the idea of having her in my bed every night appealed to me.

First, though, I had to buy a proper bed. I bought the Airstream trailer brand new, the exterior gleaming, the interior so clean I took my boots off before I entered. Winona had known what my purchase meant the instant she saw it, and she had always jokingly called it her aluminum engagement ring.

I drew her skull from its nest in the box and cupped

it in my hands. In the dark, I could not see the two fissures, at the back of her head and at the temple. My thumb sought them out, though, and I gently rubbed those old wounds.

I had never known how to love someone. When I allowed myself the honesty, I was not certain that what I felt for her now was love. What I felt for her now was a sharp twist of shame at never knowing how to give her the love she needed and a razor's edge at the remembered resentment and anger I had felt for her in the end for having needed that from me.

So I gave her what I had to give. Obsession.

"Love pales in comparison," I said quietly to the skull in my hands.

There was no sense of movement, just a sudden feeling of being watched. I looked up and met the white wolf's gaze. She stood in the center of the meadow, where my Airstream had once been parked. Moonlight gleamed against her fur and in her eyes.

Frank gave a bark of greeting and loped across the meadow to her side. He had found an old ball, and he dropped it at her feet. She merely looked at the toy before gazing back at me.

"You showed yourself to the girl, too," I said.

She did not startle at my voice. She did not tilt her head as a dog might have done. She continued to watch me.

"Did you send her to me?" I asked.

She offered no response, though the part of me that questioned whether she was real or not half expected one.

She let Frank entice her into play, but often she

stopped and turned back to me, moonlight catching in her eyes.

While Frank and the white wolf roamed the meadow together, I sat in the dark with my wife's skull cradled in my hands. The smell of wildfires in Yellowstone carried on the breeze. Summer was swift and fleeting in this area of the country. The night air was already leaning toward winter with an edge of chill to it.

My cell phone rang, shrill in the quiet. Just as startling as I fumbled in my pocket for my phone was the faint wail of sirens from the state road two miles down the canyon.

I paused when I saw who was calling. I barely had one bar of signal here, but it was enough to answer.

"Meet me at the hospital in Livingston," Jack said, voice tight. He said no more before hanging up.

My thoughts flashed to the girl, and my heart immediately jolted.

"Frank!" I called.

I glanced across the meadow and found him running toward me. The white wolf stood at the fringes of the trees. She held my gaze for a long moment before turning and disappearing into the night.

Seventeen

ANNIE

My hands were still trembling after dinner as I washed the dishes. Betty and Ed had both tried to dissuade me, saying I didn't need to clean up, but I needed something to do.

The water was warm, the dish soap making it feel like an oil slick. The sleeves of my sweatshirt were damp because they kept slipping down my forearms no matter how many times I shoved them up over my elbows. Betty and Ed were at the table discussing parts he needed to order for the auto shop.

I rinsed a plate and placed it in the drying rack. The normality of the evening felt so wonderfully foreign. In this house, it was too easy to imagine that I was part of a family.

"Jack should be on his way over," Ed said. I paused in scrubbing a pan. "Hector asked him to stay here with us after what happened earlier."

What happened earlier with me. I sucked in a breath. I was putting Ed and Betty in danger just by being here, when they had been nothing but kind to me.

"I can leave," I whispered, even though everything in me wanted to stay.

My words were met with silence. My heart sank, thinking they were debating about how to gently agree with me.

"You'll do no such thing," Ed said.

"But—"

"You're staying here with us," he said, interrupting me. His voice was firm. "You're family. That's that."

You're family. My heart clenched on those words. I wasn't. Not really. But if Betty knew the truth, Ed did as well, and he still claimed me as family. Family was what I had always loved best, and it kept being chipped away from me.

It took me a moment to feel the needling sensation of being watched. I looked up and jolted in surprise. Through the window over the sink, I had a clear view of the backyard—and the darkly dressed figure standing at the edge of the tree line. I leaned closer to the window, squinting. I couldn't tell if it was a man or a woman. Whoever it was, they were clad in darkness. I could not see a hint of skin or hair, simply a dark shadow against the deeper shadow of the woods. It looked like they carried a stick.

I was backlit in the window, I realized, clearly visible to whoever was watching. I dropped the plate I was washing back in the sink and took a quick step to the side. I flicked the light switch, plunging the kitchen into darkness.

"What—?"

"There's someone out there," I whispered urgently.

"Someone where?" Ed asked, standing.

"Outside. There's someone watching." A chill worked its way up my spine, and I moved to Betty's side. She caught my hand in her own.

"It might be Jack. Stay right here, and—"

A sound like the crack of an ax against wood interrupted Ed. Glass shattered, and Ed grunted before he fell. Betty used her grip on my hand to drag me to the floor after her. I didn't realize I was screaming until she placed her hand over my mouth.

"Quiet," she urged.

I swallowed the scream that burned in my throat. It was not a stick I had seen, I realized, but a gun. I scrambled across the floor to Ed's side. Glass from the shattered window bit into my hands and knees.

"Ed," I sobbed as I bent over him. I couldn't see where he was hit, and I was terrified to touch him.

He groaned. Betty crawled to his other side, and he reached out and grasped her wrist. "Call 9-1-1." His voice was faint and shaken. She nodded and crawled away.

Another shot cracked over us, and I ducked, pressing my head to Ed's chest. I could feel dampness against the side of my face.

"What can I do?" I whispered.

"Run."

I shook my head vehemently. "I won't leave you. Do you have a gun?"

"In the bedroom," he breathed. "Shotgun. Top of… closet."

"Shells?"

"Top…" He sucked in a breath, and I could hear a gurgling wetness in it. "Top drawer. Bed…side table."

"I'll be right back," I promised.

I shoved to my feet and ran, ducking when a shot blasted the doorframe beside my head. Splinters of wood bit into my cheek. I took the stairs three at a time. I burst into their bedroom, the door slamming into the wall with a sound like a bullet.

The shelf in the closet was high, too high for me to reach. I darted back into the bedroom to drag the bench ottoman at the end of the bed into the closet. I scrambled onto the ottoman, feeling along the top shelf until I encountered the cool, smooth barrel of the shotgun.

As I climbed down from my perch, glass broke downstairs, soon followed by the sound of Betty crying out. I stood frozen, and then the quiet creak of footsteps reached me.

I crept to the nightstand and pulled open the top drawer. The wood groaned at the movement, and my fingers shook as I searched within. When I felt the box, I yanked it free. The edge caught on the lip of the drawer, and I lost my grip on the box. It fell to the floor, shells spilling free and rolling across the hardwood.

Downstairs, I heard the footsteps pause.

I dropped to my hands and knees, scrabbling frantically under the bed for the shotgun shells.

The bottom stair creaked and then the fourth step up whined as whoever was in the house climbed the stairs.

My heart was galloping in my ears. I sprawled on my stomach and dove halfway under the bed.

I was tempted to hide, to cower in the shadows deep under the bed. My hand hit several shells. I snagged them before they could roll away.

I scrambled from beneath the bed and grabbed the shotgun. It was a pump action. I had three shells. I loaded two shells in the tube, pumped the action to chamber a shell, and slid the last into the tube.

I crouched beside the bed and lifted my head cautiously to peer at the doorway. It was dark and empty, but a floorboard creaked in the hallway at the top of the stairs.

Don't hold your breath, and aim for the chest. That had been my grandmother's advice when she taught me to shoot.

I rested the long barrel of the shotgun on the edge of the mattress, steadying my aim. I didn't look away from the doorway. I felt a trickle of dampness on my forehead, and my hands were slick, with blood or sweat, I was not certain which. I didn't remove my finger from the trigger.

As soon as the shadow darkened the doorway, I squeezed the trigger. The recoil knocked me backward, and I squeezed the trigger again as I fell.

I could hear the sound of scrambling in the hallway and then a pounding down the stairs as the intruder ran. I staggered to my feet, clutching the shotgun to my chest, and ran. I turned the corner at the bottom of the stairs just in time to see the figure clad from head to toe in black disappear through the back door.

I bolted after the intruder but skidded to a halt in the middle of the kitchen. Betty lay crumpled over Ed. Even in the dark, I could see the black stain of blood on the side of her head.

"No, no, no," I whimpered. I dropped to my knees

beside them and placed the shotgun on the floor.

I eased Betty off of Ed and rolled her to her back. Her chest rose and fell steadily, but she did not wake when I called her name.

Blood pumped steadily from the bullet hole high on Ed's chest. I grabbed the dish towel hanging on the oven handle and pressed it over the wound, leaning my weight into him to try to slow the bleeding.

"It's going to be okay," I said to the silent, dark room. "Everything is going to be okay."

Red and blue lights suddenly lit the night. "Help!" I screamed. "I need help!"

The next hours were a blur of police and paramedics, riding in the back of the ambulance, and then sitting in the corner of the waiting room at the hospital.

My hands were clutched in my lap. A paramedic had used butterfly strips on the cut on my forehead and on my arms. They had cleaned my hands and removed the slivers of glass from my palms. Ed's blood had dried brown around my nails, though.

Jack paced the far side of the waiting room. He had burst through the doors within minutes of me being ushered into the waiting room.

Betty had gained consciousness on the ambulance ride to the hospital. She had been struck in the head with the butt of a rifle. She had received a number of stitches, and they had taken her back for scans and tests an hour ago.

Ed was still in surgery. I had not missed the grimness on the paramedics' faces as they had wheeled him away from me and barred me from riding in the ambulance carrying him.

A doctor came through the double doors at the end of the hall, and Jack hurried toward him. I stood, wrapping my arms around myself. The doctor spoke quietly to Jack. I watched the body language of both men closely. When Jack's shoulders slumped, my gaze darted to the doctor, obviously a surgeon still in scrubs. He smiled and rested a hand on Jack's shoulder.

I sagged. Ed had to be alright if the surgeon was smiling.

The automatic doors at the entrance sighed behind me, and I turned to find Hector striding into the hospital. A tremor worked its way through me. He wore his usual scowl. I had never been so glad to see someone. My vision blurred when he caught sight of me and moved in my direction.

"You okay, kid?" he asked when he reached me.

My chin trembled so hard I couldn't answer. I stepped into him, planting my forehead against his chest. He froze, and I knew I should step away. He wasn't my father.

But just leaning my forehead against his chest made something burst inside me. The first sob that escaped was so raw it hurt my throat. The ones that followed were jagged and rough. My face was hot, my chest ached, and when I felt Hector tentatively cup the back of my head in his hand, I only cried harder.

Eighteen

HECTOR

"It's all my fault," she said. Her words were muffled and waterlogged, but I could interpret them.

I patted her back. "Take a deep breath now. None of this is your fault."

She tilted her head back, and her red-rimmed eyes met mine. "I'm not your daughter." A slew of tears spilled down her cheeks. "I'm not Emma."

"I know."

Her chin trembled. "My name is Annie." She stepped back and scrubbed the heels of her bandaged hands across her eyes. "I saw you on the news. You were being interviewed about shutting down that senator's poaching ring." She took a deep breath, and it caught and warbled in her throat. "You broke the senator's jaw and got away with it. I…I needed someone like that, like you."

"For what?" I asked, but I was not certain she heard me.

"I looked you up. I read about what happened to your wife and daughter. I didn't mean to say I was your daughter. I just wanted you to listen to me."

She gulped back sobs. I remembered that day when she had shown up at the inn and then again at the liquor store. I had shut her down and not given her the opportunity to explain why she sought me out.

"I just need…" She swallowed and dragged her forearm across her face.

If she were Emma, I would want someone to take her in, make certain she was safe, and give her anything she needed. "What do you need?" I asked.

Her throat worked. "Help," she whispered. "I need help."

"Hector."

I turned at my name and saw Jack at the end of the hall.

I led the girl to a chair in the waiting area. "Sit right here. After I see to things here, we'll talk." She shivered, and I stripped off my jacket and draped it around her shoulders.

"They're putting Mom in a room," Jack said as I approached him.

"Ed?"

"They just finished surgery. He's going to be moved to ICU." He paced the room the nurse led us to as if the walls were cages. "My parents have no enemies. I can't think of anyone who would want to do this to them."

"What about your enemies?" He and I had a long history of antagonism and distrust. Several months ago, when I discovered my wife had uncovered a poaching ring run from Senator Grant Larson's ranch, Jack had been the one to pull the plug on the operation after I lost my head and attacked the senator. He had also been the one to save me when Larson ordered his men to kill me. "You worked for Larson. Has there been fall out since he was arrested?"

He shook his head. "The men he hired for security weren't loyal to him, just to the paycheck. They rolled up camp as soon as the feds showed up. The ranch is an operation itself, and a well-run one, even without Larson's oversight. He hired good men in that regard."

"Any tension at the new job?" I asked.

He had hired on after leaving Larson with a local helicopter touring agency. "None." He rubbed the back of his neck. "Look, I didn't try to discourage Mom and Pop from taking her in. Mainly because neither of them would listen to me. But that girl is hiding something, something big."

"I know," I said.

"Something that almost got my mother killed, and my father barely made it off the operating table," he said, biting off the words. "This is her doing. She lied about being Emma, and now this. I won't—"

Betty's voice cut him off sharply as she was wheeled into the room. I did not understand the words she said to him in Lakota, but I understood the tone and Jack's reaction. He paced to the window and stood with his back to the room, shoulders tense.

I stood back as the nurses settled Betty into the hospital bed. She had battled cancer twice since my girls had gone missing. I had learned of this third and final fight the beginning of the year.

In the fifteen years since Winona and Emma had disappeared, I had seen Betty only a handful of times. Our paths rarely crossed. Winona and I had been married six months when she brought me home to introduce me to her family. Family was a foreign concept to me. My mother was a drunk who choked to death on her own vomit when I was just a boy. The rancher who had offered me a job had been tough but fair. The taciturn man was the closest thing I had to a father, and when he died several years after taking me in, I had borrowed his surname as I set out on my own again.

I had never been around families, and if I were completely honest with myself, a small sliver of what might have been hope had worked its way like a splinter into me at Winona's excitement to introduce me to her parents and brother. The splinter had festered quickly. Her parents had been carefully polite, but I could see the disapproval in their tight expressions. I was not good enough for their daughter.

Winona had leaned her head against my shoulder when we left. "Don't worry," she said. "They'll come around."

They had not, but I had not exactly done anything to encourage a change of opinion of me either. Whereas Ed's disappointment in his daughter's choice in husbands had become vocal over the years, Betty had never said anything directly to me. She simply studied me with that penetrating gaze.

She did so now, and when the nurses left, assured of her comfort for the moment, she surprised me by holding out her hand. I hesitated, but she waited me out. She had withered away over the years, reduced to little more than bone. Her headscarf was gone, and a line of staples along the side of her head glinted in the light. When I first met her, her hair was a long, black curtain she kept in a neat braid. What little had grown back in tufts on her head was white, and I could see they had carefully shaved a section where she had needed staples.

Her arm trembled, as if it were an effort for her to hold it up. I crossed the room and carefully took her extended hand.

"She needs you," she said, and though her voice was weak in sound, I could hear the steely undercurrent of the tone. "Emma needs you desperately."

"She's not Emma," Jack began, but a quick cut of Betty's gaze silenced him.

"She's someone's Emma," I said.

Betty nodded, and the tension in her face eased. Her hand felt frail in mine, and I held it carefully, afraid I would inadvertently break her brittle fingers. Her grip on my hand was strong, though. "She's in danger. That woman tonight—"

"A woman did this to you?" I interrupted.

"She knew my name," she whispered. "I grabbed a knife but I wasn't strong enough to stop her. She said, 'I don't want to hurt you, Betty.'"

"Did you recognize her voice?" I asked.

Her eyes slid closed, and the lines around her eyes tightened. "No, it happened so quickly, and I was afraid."

Jack abandoned his station at the window and came to the opposite side of the bed, resting his hand on his mother's shoulder. "You don't have to be afraid any longer, Mom. You're safe."

She opened her eyes, but she did not spare her son a glance. She looked right at me. "I'm afraid for her,

Hector. She needs you to protect her."

I dropped my gaze to our clasped hands. I had failed all those years ago. Failed at loving my girls and failed at protecting them. I would never get another chance with them. Even if I did, I was not certain I wouldn't fail again.

"I didn't know how to be a husband or a father."

When Betty squeezed my fingers, I realized I had said the words aloud.

"We didn't give you a chance to be part of our family," she said. I lifted my gaze to hers and saw that her eyes glistened. "I'm sorry."

Pressure built behind my eyes. I tried to speak, but my voice caught in my throat.

"She's not our Emma," she said, voice soft. "But you're not the man you were fifteen years ago."

Nineteen

ANNIE

I sat huddled in Hector's jacket waiting for him to appear through the double doors. There was so much I needed to tell him, needed to show him.

My backpack. I jolted. In the chaos, I had forgotten my backpack.

I lurched to my feet and hurried to the front desk.

The receptionist smiled at me tiredly. "May I help you?"

"The man who just came in a few minutes ago," I said quickly. "I need you to give him a message when he comes back."

I relayed the message and then ran outside.

The parking lot was quiet. I spotted Hector's truck in the lot. Frank sat in the passenger's seat watching me. I patted the pockets of Hector's jacket. They were empty. He must have his keys on him. If I wanted him to trust me, if I wanted him to help me, I couldn't steal his truck.

But I needed to get back to the house and get my backpack. It may not even still be there. I could only hope that if the intruder had waited until the house was empty, my hiding place had gone undiscovered. All the proof I had was contained in that backpack.

There was a gas station across the street from the hospital with a lone SUV at one of the pumps.

I hurried toward the man as he replaced the nozzle and screwed the gas cap back on.

"Excuse me!" I called.

He turned. He was younger than I had thought he was from behind. "Yeah?"

"I need to get to Raven's Gap as soon as possible. Can I get a ride?" I asked. When he hesitated, I lied. "I can pay you."

He looked me up and down. He smiled, and I almost changed my mind. "Sure. Hop in."

You have to get the backpack, I reminded myself when my feet remained rooted to the pavement. Unease made my stomach tight as I climbed into the passenger's seat. There were empty beer bottles littering the floorboard, and the smell of the interior made my nose wrinkle.

"Thanks," I said. "My dad is expecting me home."

He darted a smile in my direction as he put the SUV in gear. "Don't worry. I'll get you home."

I didn't bother with the seatbelt, and I sat close against the door, keeping my fingers on the handle. He turned in the right direction once he reached the highway.

I jumped when his hand left the wheel suddenly, but he just fiddled with the dial on the radio.

"You like country music?" he asked.

I watched him closely from the corner of my eye.

The interior of the vehicle was dark, and his face looked warped in the glow from dash.

"It's fine," I said. "My dad likes it. He's expecting me."

"Hm," was his only response.

The twangy music filled the cab. As the miles rolled by, I forced myself not to relax, even though his hands remained on the steering wheel tapping out the beat. He never made a move to turn in the wrong direction. The only thing out of his mouth was the occasional out of tune warble of a line from a song on the radio.

A truck passed us going the opposite direction, and from the corner of my eye, I saw his head turn. He studied me in the glow of oncoming lights and then he turned to study the road again.

"There's a case of beer in the backseat," he said. "Why don't you have one?"

"No, thanks," I said, voice sharp.

"Ah, come on now. Don't be like that."

"I'm not old enough to drink." I shifted so my fingers could brush against the door handle.

"Well, I won't tell if you won't." His tone was soft and coaxing. It raised the hair on my arms.

I remained silent, and he shifted in his seat, muttering under his breath. I stared at the road, throat tight, heart knocking. It was too many miles to Raven's Gap.

I counted the seconds that passed. It was fifteen minutes before he said suddenly, "Show me the money you have on you."

"What?"

"You said you would pay me," he said. "Show me how much cash you have."

I swallowed. "Why don't you just pull over and let

me out here?"

His hand landed on my knee, hard and heavy. His fingers dug into my skin when I tried to jerk away.

"You don't have any money, do you, you lying little bitch?" Gone was the soft and coaxing. Now his tone was mean.

I yanked at his wrist. "Get your hands off me."

"There are other ways of paying me," he said, and his hard hand shifted from my knee to my thigh.

"Fuck you," I snapped. I dug my fingernails hard into the flesh of his wrist and gouged deep furrowed scratches into his arm.

He shouted and released me as suddenly as he had grabbed me. He slammed on the brakes, and I threw my hands out to save myself from hitting the dash face first.

"You'll pay for that!" he yelled, and lunged across the console.

I snagged a glass bottle from the floor and broke it on the dash. I had it at his throat the moment his hands landed in my hair. He yanked me toward him but froze when the broken glass pierced his skin.

"I'll slit you ear to ear if you don't get your hands off me and let me out of this car," I whispered.

His hands tightened in my hair. My wounded scalp burned and strained against his hold. I pushed the edge of the broken bottle harder against his throat and felt his skin give.

He released me so quickly I had to catch myself from falling into him.

I did not take my gaze off of him as I reached blindly behind me and fumbled for the door handle. Only when I had shoved the door open did I ease up the pressure on his throat. I scrambled backward, and when he reached for me again, I swung my makeshift weapon, slicing his arm.

He cried out. "You fucking bitch!"

I fell backward out of the SUV, hitting the ground hard enough to drive the breath from my lungs. I struggled to my feet, breath locked in my chest. I held the broken glass bottle out in front of me, but he did not try to follow me. He spun the wheel and accelerated so sharply rubber squealed and burned.

The door slammed as he roared away, but I could still hear him screaming at me.

I staggered to the side of the road and bent double, battling to suck air into my lungs. Fury and fear paced restlessly inside me. His tail lights disappeared around the bend, and after several moments, I could no longer hear the sound of his engine.

It took much longer for me to stop shaking.

When I could breathe normally again, I straightened. The glass bottle shattered on the pavement when I dropped it. Once my legs had stopped trembling, I turned and began to run.

It was dark, but the moon was bright. The road curved ahead of me, gray in the pale light, and the river was a black snake that curled with it.

A blur of movement caught the corner of my eye. I stumbled to a halt and peered into the darkness. I couldn't see anything. My first thought was that he had circled back on foot. I leapt into a run again, heart drumming faster than my pace warranted.

The movement came again, and this time I turned

my head quickly enough. It was an animal, running along the opposite riverbank.

I stopped running and scanned the bank closely. I lost track of where I had seen the movement, but then a gleam of pale light glinted on white fur. My breath caught in my throat.

The white wolf had stopped running as well. She loped to the edge of the river and lowered her head to sniff along the edge of the water. Her head came up suddenly, and I could have sworn she looked directly at me.

She had to be the same white wolf I had seen at the inn. We stared at one another for a long moment until her head suddenly turned.

I couldn't hear anything, but she obviously did. She met my gaze once more, and then she began to lope along the riverbank.

I ran, picking up my pace. I imagined she slowed her four paws to accommodate my two feet, because for several heartbeats it felt as if we ran alongside one another on opposite banks of the river. My heart soared at the idea.

Then suddenly she veered away from the riverbank and was absorbed in the night, disappearing from view.

I stopped, peering after her, but she was gone.

The sound of an engine approaching startled me. I moved off the road, wishing I had kept the broken bottle. Moonlight blanketed the rolling flat expanse of ranch land on either side of the road. If it was that man returning, I would have no place to hide.

The lights were closer to the ground, though. It was not an SUV that approached me. When the edge of the headlights caught me in their gleam before I could move further off the road, the driver slowed.

I braced myself, ready to flee.

The passenger's side window rolled down, and a familiar voice said, "Emma? What are you doing out here in the middle of the night?"

My shoulders slumped in relief, and the tension bled out of me. I approached the car. "I'm so glad to see you," I said, and I heard the tremor in my voice that accompanied the admission.

I heard the click of the doors unlocking. I did not think twice about opening the door and sliding within.

Part II

Twenty

JOAN

then

A hand on my shoulder woke me.

"You'll want to go to the hospital," Donald said quietly.

As soon as I was awake, I knew. I could feel the life slipping from me to pool between my legs, staining our bedsheets.

I lay there for long minutes, clamping my thighs as tightly together as I could. It was useless, though. Nothing I did could stop it.

"Do you want me to call you an ambulance?"

I roused when Donald spoke again. "No," I said, voice dull. "I can drive."

He leaned over and pressed his lips to my cheek. "I'm sorry, sweetheart."

No more sorry than I was. But because this had become commonplace, he finished getting ready for his shift at the police department and left.

I did not cry as I stood in the shower and watched

the tide of red swirl down the drain. I put a towel over the seat of my car and drove to the hospital in Livingston. I was further along this time than I had ever made it before, but I did not cry over the next few hours as the doctors and nurses made certain nothing remained clinging within me. It had once been the promise of life, but now it spelled death.

I stared at the ceiling with my feet in the stirrups. I had always done everything right. I was the perfect daughter of the mayor. I was on the Nordic ski team in high school, and I had been the head cheerleader. I dated the quarterback of the football team, and we were crowned king and queen of the senior prom. I was valedictorian, and three months after graduating, I married my high school sweetheart.

I had been the perfect daughter, the perfect student, the perfect friend, and then the perfect wife. I succeeded in everything I tried.

Except for the one thing I wanted the most. In that, I was a failure.

The doctors and nurses were kind, their hands gentle, their tones sympathetic. They said the same thing I had heard numerous times before.

"It's not your fault."

"There was nothing you could have done."

Thankfully, none of them said, "Next time." They had seen my chart. They knew my odds.

When I was scraped clean and barren once more, I changed into the clean clothes I brought with me and drove home, as raw on the outside as I felt on the inside.

I stared blankly at the road before me as I drove. At

a red light, my attention wandered. I did not realize the light had changed until the car behind me laid on its horn.

I jumped and glanced in my rearview mirror. The man in the car behind me was gesturing, and I could see his lips moving as he swore at me. I put my car in park, stepped from my vehicle, and approached him.

Everything about me was perfect again. The hair, the makeup, the pencil skirt and cardigan, the heels. I was armored with lipstick and pearls.

He stopped yelling, and his hand dropped as soon as he saw me. He rolled down his window. Even though I looked perfect on the outside, something must have shown in my eyes.

When I said, "Do you have a problem, sir?" his immediate response was, "No, not at all. I'm sorry about that."

"I just wanted to be certain," I said. I returned to my car, and he sat politely behind me through another cycle of the light before it turned green again.

The two-lane highway to Raven's Gap had little traffic on it. When I saw a car approaching me on the straight stretches between ranch land, I contemplated swerving into the next lane when they were too close to be able to stop a head-on collision. I did not follow through, though.

I slowed when I saw the car abandoned on the side of the road. I recognized it, and as soon as I thought about the owner of the vehicle, I felt the numbness that had overtaken me thaw as suspicion and anger roiled beneath the surface.

I was too much of a coward to ask Donald point

blank. A coward, and embarrassed. Because we were perfect, and I could not bear to have that image destroyed.

A couple of miles ahead, I spotted her walking along the side of the road. She stood well off the shoulder. I slowed as I approached and rolled the passenger's window down.

She moved closer and smiled as she bent to peer through the window. "I cannot tell you how glad I am to see you," Winona Lewis said.

Her daughter, Emma, was propped on her hip, and the little girl waved at me as her mother spoke.

"I saw your car a couple miles back," I said, and I was pleased with how normal my voice sounded. "Is everything okay?"

She pushed her long, dark hair away from her face when the wind cast a curtain of it over her face. "I'm hoping it's not dead for good. I was heading into town to pick up the cake for Emma's party."

I hit the button for the automatic locks. "Hop in. I'll give you a ride."

She slid into the passenger's seat. "Thank you, Joan. I really appreciate it."

She turned Emma in her lap to face forward and wrapped the seatbelt around both of them. The little girl grinned at me and let loose a torrent of jabber.

Winona and I were both quiet the next few miles, and when she let out a sigh, I glanced at the clock. It was five minutes past closing time for the bakery.

"I can pick the cake up for you first thing when they open tomorrow," I offered. "I can either run it out to your place or send it home with your husband when he leaves the station."

"You wouldn't mind doing that?" she asked. "I've already paid for it."

"Not at all," I said.

She leaned her head back against the seat. "Thank you." There was something in her voice, something tired and strained. "If you just want to drop me off at my dad's shop, that would be great."

I thought about the emptiness and quiet that awaited me at my own house.

"Would you like to come over for a few minutes?" I asked. "I can make us some tea. I could use a cup today."

She hesitated. We were not close. We never had been. I wouldn't call us friends. But I always kept Donald's goals in mind and made it a point to be welcoming and polite to everyone.

I was a friendly acquaintance to everyone in town, but I realized suddenly that I had no friends, no one who would sit and cry with me, no one who would hold my hand.

I thought she would refuse. Instead, she said, "Sure. I would enjoy that."

Relief swept through me. When we reached my lane, I turned off the state road and followed the long drive home.

Twenty-One

HECTOR

The waiting room was empty.

"Sir?"

The woman at the front desk waved me over.

"Did you see the girl leave?" I demanded. "The girl who came in with the ambulance."

"Yes, sir," she said. "She left a message for you. She wanted me to tell you she had to leave right away and get back to the house. She said she has something important to show you and she forgot and left it there."

"How long has she been gone?"

"She left right after you went back," she said.

I glanced at the clock on the wall. After waiting for the results of the myriad of tests they had ordered for Betty, Jack and I had been directed to the separate waiting room for ICU to see Ed after he was wheeled in from the recovery unit.

The girl had been gone for over an hour.

I hurried out to my truck. Frank greeted me as I climbed into the cab. I passed a hand over his head as I twisted and peered out the back window, scanning the parking lot. The girl was nowhere to be seen. I had no clue how she would have gotten back to Ed and Betty's.

I kept my eyes peeled as I drove through the night, but my headlights did not illuminate her walking along the side of the road anywhere between Livingston and Raven's Gap.

The Decker house was dark when I pulled up. The police had already come and gone. Ted Peters, the forensic technician, would have done a thorough job collecting any evidence.

I sat in my truck on the curb and studied the house. The front looked as peaceful as ever, unadorned but neatly constructed.

"Let's go," I said to Frank.

We circled the house. The window over the sink and the glass pane in the back door were shot out. The knob turned easily underhand, and I reached inside, feeling along the wall until I found the switch.

The kitchen looked like all hell had broken loose within. Chairs were overturned. Splinters of wood littered the floor, and fragments of glass glinted in the light. I could see bullet holes in the cabinets, and a gouge in the doorframe leading into the hall. Blood was pooled on the tiles by the table where Ed had fallen.

The bullet had pierced his lung and missed his heart by inches. He was not out of danger, but the doctors were hopeful.

I tried to recall what the girl had told me her name was. "Annie?" Silence was the only answer.

There was no sound of movement within.

I lifted Frank into my arms and carried him over the

glass in the kitchen. In the hall, I placed him back on his feet. He followed close at my side as I traversed the stairs.

It had been a long time since I had set foot in this house. Over fifteen years now. I had always been an outsider. Never unwelcome in those first fifteen years of marriage, but not truly part of the family.

I still remembered the layout of the house, though. I was not surprised to find Ed and Betty had put the girl in Winona's old bedroom.

The bed was unmade, and I paused as I caught sight of the stuffed animal propped against the pillows. I crossed the room slowly and picked up the patched rabbit. *Chapa*. That was what Emma had called him, dragging him by the ears after her wherever she went. I fingered the velvet texture of his ears and wondered how I could have forgotten about him.

Frank caught my attention when he ducked his head under the bed, hind end in the air, tail wagging.

"What did you find?"

I knelt beside him and peered beneath the bed. A lumpen shape had been shoved halfway under, and I leaned over and caught it, dragging it from its hiding place.

I recognized it as soon as I saw it in the light. It was the girl's backpack, carried as faithfully as my daughter had carried her stuffed rabbit. I had never seen her without the backpack.

This must have been what she left the hospital to retrieve.

I unzipped the largest pocket and peered within. I was not certain what I had expected. Perhaps cash, drugs, stolen items, the gear of a teenage girl.

Instead, the bag was stuffed with file folders. I searched the other large compartment of the backpack and found it contained the same. In the small pocket, I found several sheets of paper neatly folded.

My knees ached from kneeling on the floor. I groaned as I moved to sit on the bed. I paused in unfolding the sheets of paper.

They were printouts from news articles. The first one was dated from January, the second from April. I skimmed the news articles. The first detailed the death of Jeff Roosevelt and the discovery of the bodies of his numerous victims. The second covered the arrest of Senator Grant Larson and the law enforcement crackdown on the multi-million-dollar trophy hunting operation he had been running from his ranch.

My name was mentioned in both articles.

I flipped to the third article. It was fifteen years old, and seeing it again had the same effect it had when I first read it. It was the first article written about Winona and Emma after their disappearance.

I refolded the news articles and stuffed them back in the bag.

I searched through the drawers and closet. The backpack was what she would have returned to the house for. There was nothing else in the room that was hers.

I pulled out my cell phone and dialed Jack's number. When he answered, I said, "Has Annie returned to the hospital?"

"Who?"

"The girl," I said. "She left me a message at the reception desk saying she needed to return to the house."

"To Mom and Pop's? How the hell would she have gotten back?" Jack asked.

"She didn't," I said. I glanced at the backpack. "She never made it."

He was silent for a beat. "I'll check the lobby." I waited as he moved through the hospital, his footsteps ringing hollowly in the halls. After several minutes, he finally spoke. "She's not here."

"Shit." I glanced around the room. "*Shit*."

"Do you need me to come help?"

"No," I said. "Stay with Ed and Betty. It may be nothing, so don't tell them I can't find the girl. They don't need that on their minds right now. Call me if she shows up at the hospital."

"I'll keep an eye out," he promised.

It could be nothing. The kid could be safe and sound. The unease raising the hair on the back of my neck could be for no reason.

I need help. The plaintive note in her tearful voice rang in my ears.

I was an old man haunted by ghosts, but I had learned a long time ago to listen to my instincts. Right now, my instincts said something was wrong. My instincts said the kid was in trouble.

Frank whined, sensing my mood, and rested his chin on my knee.

I stared into his eyes. "Not again," I said, and he lifted his muzzle from my knee and tilted his head. "Let's go find her."

He bounded into the hallway. I snagged the girl's backpack and followed him.

Only when we were back in the truck and I was pulling away from the curb did I realize I still carried my daughter's worn stuffed rabbit.

Twenty-Two

Joan

now

The nightmares had plagued me for fifteen years. They had changed as soon as she came to town, though. It was no longer simply memories that haunted me.

The crying child in my memories that startled me from sleep so often morphed into something that disturbed me even more. Now, a small, skeletal hand reaching for mine accompanied the cry. When I tried to pull away, the boney fingers latched onto my hand in a grip I could not break no matter how hard I struggled.

I never screamed for help in the nightmare. I woke with my face damp and an apology on my lips every time the clutching grip on my fingers suddenly yanked me into a dark hole in the ground.

Donald had given up sleeping with me years ago. I knew he was disgusted with me, and he had no patience for my fears.

The other day when I overheard someone mention Hector's daughter had returned, I slipped away from the reception desk and hurried to Donald's office. He barely spared me a glance when I closed and locked his office door behind me.

"She's back," I whispered, and sank into the chair across from his desk. My legs would not hold me up any longer.

"Who?" he asked without looking up from what he was working on.

It felt as if my throat were closing. "Emma."

His head came up at that. "That's impossible."

My head was shaking on a constant swivel. "She's here. In town. She came back. She's here for me. I know it. After I—"

"*Joan*." His voice was as hard as a blow, and I jumped and flinched. "Shut *up*," he snapped. "I want you to remember where we are, and keep your fucking mouth shut."

"Donald." My whisper shook.

"Enough," he said. The tight ticking in his jaw and his white knuckles made my stomach tighten. "You're worked up over nothing. Whoever this girl is, she's lying. Now go fix your face and take a pill. You're a wreck."

"Donald," I tried again.

I shrank under his gaze. He was a different man from the one I married. When I married him, he had been ambitious, but he had also been kind and had genuinely cared about making a difference. After his four years in the Marines, he had gone straight to the police academy.

Sometimes I no longer recognized the man before me. But then, I had trouble recognizing myself in the mirror as well. Secrets like ours—like *mine*—wore heavily.

"Let it go," he said slowly in a voice that brooked no argument.

But I found that I could not.

I had not set out to run her over the other day when she was crossing the street. I told myself I was just watching, but then my foot had fallen on the accelerator and I stared at her as she loomed closer and closer in the windshield until she leapt out of the way at the last minute.

When I saw her fleeing the swarm of reporters, I rescued her. I remembered Donald's words, that she had to be lying, she could not be Emma.

She looked just like Winona, though. The long, dark hair, the midnight eyes. She even smiled the same way, kindly but with a slant of sadness.

I didn't have to kill her, I reasoned as she sat in my office yesterday. I could just frighten her away, ensure she was gone before she remembered what I had done.

With the rifle in my hand, though, I realized how easy it would be to end it. Maybe then she would cease haunting me.

I hadn't meant to shoot Ed, and I made certain I didn't hit Betty too hard. I had not expected Emma to be armed, though. If I were taller, the shotgun blast would have taken my head off.

Now, as my headlights illuminated her standing off the side of the road, I considered my original reaction again. A hit and run would be tragic, and it would solve everything.

Instead, I found myself slowing to a halt and rolling down my window.

There was such a strong feeling of déjà vu as Emma slid into the passenger's seat that it left me dizzy. I wondered if she felt the same.

I forced myself to take a deep breath and relaxed my grip on the steering wheel as she buckled her seatbelt.

I wondered why she was on the side of the road in the middle of the night, but I did not ask. "I'll take you to the inn."

Hector as a father was something I had a hard time imagining. I had never intentionally set out to have an affair with the man, but one night after Donald had been brutal with his fists, I left the house and drove. I had no destination in mind. I thought I drove aimlessly. Until I turned down the narrow, hard-packed dirt road that led up the canyon to the sprawling plot of land he owned.

When I reached his Airstream, I sat in my car for a long time, wondering what I was doing there. He opened the door and stood on the cinderblock front step with his rifle casually propped on his shoulder.

I got out of the car carefully, wincing. My side hurt with every breath, and I wrapped an arm around my ribcage to ease the sharp ache as I approached him. I stood in the spill of light from the trailer for a long moment while he did nothing more than study me.

Finally, he set the rifle aside and gestured to my face. "Looks like you could use some ice for that."

My fingers came up to my face. I winced as I touched the tender warmth of my cheekbone. Donald was usually so careful not to leave marks that anyone could see.

"I fell into a doorframe," I said, and shame slid through me.

I had crossed paths with Hector at the police department. He struck me as a gruff, borderline rude man who still managed to have a magnetism about him that drew the eye. He also spoke more plainly than anyone I had ever met.

"No need to lie to me, Joan. I know the bastard hits you," he said. "Come inside if you like. I'll get you an ice pack."

He disappeared inside, and I followed him.

I took him by surprise later when I kissed him.

He set me away from him immediately. "You don't need to do that."

I had been so curious about him in the last five years. I had never imagined the blame and suspicion that would be heaped on him. I loved my hometown, but I knew how closed off we were to outsiders. He had never been welcomed with open arms, and since Winona and Emma had disappeared, he had withdrawn even more.

He was too rough and rugged to ever be handsome, but as I looked up at him, I could not deny how appealing he was in that rawboned, windburned way. Didn't I owe him a little, and didn't I deserve to be touched with gentleness again?

I placed my hand on his chest, right over his heart, and I felt the steady, unhurried rhythm against my palm.

"I want to," I said.

He had not denied me then or in the countless times I had gone to him since that night.

"Will you take me to Ed and Betty's?" Emma said suddenly as we reached the outskirts of Raven's Gap. I jumped at the sound of her voice. "I need to get something there. It's important. Hect—My dad knows where I'm going to be and is going to meet me there."

Had I dropped something at their house? Had she seen me?

She had to remember something, from tonight or from that day fifteen years ago.

Twenty-Three

HECTOR

The girl was not in the spare room adjoining mine.

I crossed to the guest room side of the inn and pounded on the door to Evelyn's room. There was no answer.

I lifted my fist to hammer again at her door but then paused. Nothing but silence greeted me from the other side of the door. No scuff of movement, no curious call, no sudden flair of light bleeding under the seam of the door. I considered how a woman would interpret a heavy knock on her door in the dark of night.

"Evelyn, it's Hector," I said, voice low, my head bent close to the door. I could imagine her creeping silently from her bed in the dark and standing on the opposite side of the door, holding her breath. "I can't find the—" I caught myself. "I can't find Emma."

I knew my assumption was correct when the door immediately opened.

"I didn't see her this evening," she said, "and I just closed up the inn an hour ago."

I told her of the events for the night.

She pushed her glasses up her nose. "Let me change. I'll help you look."

While she headed out to canvas the town, I went straight to Maggie's.

I knew Maggie kept a loaded shotgun in the corner of her bedroom, so when I pounded on her front door, I called, "It's me, Maggie."

When she did not answer immediately, I knocked again, even louder. Louie began to bark at the back of the house. Frank's ears perked up and he responded in kind.

The day Winona and Emma disappeared, I had arrived home seven hours after my shift ended. There had been a multi-vehicle accident with five fatalities on the state road north of Gardiner, and the county had called in every available officer to help. I had arrived home exhausted and irritable, and I had forgotten to pick up the cake Winona had ordered for Emma's birthday party.

When Winona had asked me to go back to the bakery for it, I snapped at her. Our last interaction had been one of frustration and anger. We had argued, and while I retreated into the minuscule bathroom in the Airstream to wash away the grime of the day, she left with Emma to return to town. I had never seen them again.

After showering, I had fallen in bed and slept for ten hours straight. I woke to a silent, empty trailer. It was the middle of the night. Winona was not in bed beside me and the crib attached to her side of the bed was empty.

I sat on the cinder block that served as our front

stoop and drank a beer. I had not wondered much at Winona and Emma's absence, though it was unusual. No matter how angry and frustrated Winona became with me, she always slept at my side. But the distance between us was a rift that kept drifting farther apart. I thought she may have stayed with her parents, since Emma's birthday party was to be held at their house later in the day.

I finished my beer and took a pain pill from the stash I kept hidden from Winona. She did not like that I still took them years after I had healed from my injuries.

I did not bother telling her that they were as good at dulling mental pain as they were physical.

When I woke again, someone was pounding on the front door of the Airstream. For a groggy moment, I thought I had slept through Emma's birthday party. I stumbled to the door and found Donald Marsden on my cinder block stoop. He had been a detective then, aiming to climb the political ladder within the police department.

"It's Winona and Emma," he said.

The door in front of me swung open, jerking me back to the present.

Maggie clutched her robe around her and rubbed sleep from her eyes. "Hector, what on earth is going on? It's the middle of the night."

"It's Emma," I said. I blinked, dragged back fifteen years. I corrected myself. "Annie. The girl. She's gone."

I felt the same crushing pressure I had felt thirty years ago on the dirty floor of the arena. Maggie grabbed my hand, grounding me.

"We'll find her," she assured me.

While Evelyn and Maggie combed Raven's Gap street by street, I retraced the route to the hospital in Livingston.

I drove slowly, scanning the shoulders of the two-lane state road. When there was no shoulder and the road dropped off steeply, I pulled over and walked along the route, directing my flashlight into the gorges and ravines. Frank caught no trace of her scent in those stretches, and I spotted nothing.

I stopped in Gardiner and every small outpost between there and the hospital. No one at the service stations or elsewhere had seen a young girl matching Annie's description.

When my phone rang and the screen showed Maggie's number, I answered quickly. "Anything?"

"We haven't found a trace of her, Hec," she said. Concern was thick in her voice.

"We'll find her." *Not again.* The words circled in my head like vultures.

When I reached the hospital, it was mid-morning. I pulled into the gas station on the opposite side of the street.

"I only came on shift a couple of hours ago," the woman behind the counter said when I questioned her about seeing Annie last night. "But I can call the night manager and see if he remembers anything."

I nodded, and several minutes later she thrust the phone toward me.

"Yes?" I asked.

"Angela said you were asking about seeing a teenage girl last night?" the voice on the other end of the line asked.

"Sometime between eleven and midnight, roughly," I confirmed. "Probably closer to eleven."

"She an Indian?"

"American Indian," I confirmed.

"I don't know if it was the same girl you're looking for, but I did see a teenager come up and start talking to a man who was outside pumping gas. She got in the car with him and left."

"What time?"

"Just like you said, right around eleven," the man said.

"You have security footage?" I asked.

"Yes. Just ask Angela to roll the feed back for you."

I handed the phone back to the woman behind the counter. She listened on the line for a moment, and then she hung up and gestured for me to follow her.

"The computer is in the back room," she said.

Moments later, I watched on screen as Annie approached a man standing beside his vehicle at the gas pump. As the car pulled away from the service station with Annie in the passenger's seat, I said, "Pause the image there."

I grabbed my phone and dialed the police department's number. Joan Marsden answered on the fourth ring.

"It's me," I said.

There was silence on the other end of the line for a long beat. "Is something wrong?" Her voice was pitched low.

"I need you to run a plate for me."

"You know I can't do that," she said.

"Please," I said, and I was surprised to hear myself say the word. At her indrawn breath, I thought she might have been just as stunned. "It's about An—" I cut myself off. "It's about Emma. I can't find her, and the last time she was spotted was when she was getting into this vehicle last night."

"You can't find her?"

"I don't have time to explain," I said.

"Okay," she whispered. "Okay, give me just a moment."

"I'll wait." I repeated the license plate to her.

In a matter of seconds, she said, "It's a silver 4Runner?"

"That's it," I confirmed.

"It is registered to a Chris Samford." She rattled off an address local to Livingston.

It took me ten minutes to find the address she had given me. The house was derelict, the machinery parts in the yard rusted. The place had a look of abandonment, aside from the silver 4Runner parked beside the house.

I told Frank to stay in the truck and strode through the overgrowth to the front porch. I was surprised it did not collapse under me as I pounded on the front door.

There was no sound from within. I knocked harder.

"Jesus!" a voice cried out within. "Who the fuck is it?"

"I'm looking for the girl you picked up at the gas station across from the hospital last night."

The door was yanked open, and the stale air of the interior rolled out to greet me. It smelled like sweat and beer and piss. Or that might have been the belligerent man in front of me.

"Whatever she told you I did, it's a damn lie," he said.

I said nothing. I simply stared at the man.

He was young, but he was going to seed. His gut was beginning to droop over his belt, and his skin had a yellow tint from too little sunlight and too much alcohol. A bandage brown with blood was wrapped around his forearm.

He dropped his gaze. "Look, all I did was give her a ride. When she came up to me at the gas station, she told me she could pay me. But then when we got farther down the road, she said she didn't have any money."

"And what did you do?"

He flinched. "Nothing, man. I swear. I mean, yeah, I told her I would accept payment of a different kind. But I didn't."

Immediately, rage darkened my vision. My hands started to shake, and I wondered at the sudden surge of fury like I had never felt before.

He must have seen part of what I was feeling on my face, because his words fell over one another in his rush to speak. "I put my hand on her knee, that's all, I swear. I let her out of my car a few miles north of Gardiner, right before Yankee Jim Canyon."

"You assaulted a young girl, a minor, and then you abandoned her on the side of the road in the middle of the night."

I spoke slowly and deliberately, and he clutched at the door, ready to slam it in my face. I slid my foot forward to block his escape plan.

His face took on a mean, mulish expression. "I got nothin' else to say to you. I didn't do anything to her. If she says I did, she's lyin'."

"Alright." I held out my hand. "Thank you for your time and for the information."

He stared at me, perplexed at the change of tone. He reached out and clasped my hand, shaking it. "Sure. No problem."

My hand clenched around his. His eyes went wide, and the fucker squeaked in alarm when he tried to yank his hand away and could not.

I waited until he met my gaze. "This is for putting your hand on her."

"Wait, wait, man, I—"

He screamed as I snapped his wrist with a quick twist and jerk.

I let go, and he crumbled to his knees in the doorway, squealing like a pig. I stared down at him for a long moment as he sniveled and whined and cursed. I was tempted to grab his greasy hair and bash his head against the doorframe.

A bark from the truck snagged my attention, and I turned away.

"If I find out you did more than put your hand on her, I'll be back. Next time, it'll be your neck I break," I called over my shoulder.

Frank stared at me, tail wagging, mouth hanging open in a canine grin, as I climbed back in the truck. "You should have let me kill him," I told the poodle as I threw the truck in reverse. I was surprised to feel my hands shaking against the wheel and gearshift.

Frank made no argument for his interference. He simply settled at my side and rested his head on the stuffed rabbit lying on the seat between us.

Twenty-Four

Joan

then

This had been a mistake.

I stared at Emma, watching the careful way she picked up a berry between her thumb and forefinger, studying the delighted surprise on her face when the berry slipped from her finger and bounced across the table. She reared back, dipping her head back against Winona's chest to peer up at her mother, grinning and jabbering in that intelligible way young children had.

I looked away and pressed a hand against my chest. *Could hearts actually break?* I wondered. Because mine felt as if it had been splintered over and over again until it was barely managing to pump.

"Joan," Winona said softly.

Her hand covered mine on the table, warm and calloused and strong. I blinked and realized I had been staring blindly across the room. My face was damp. I palmed away the tears that were leaking from my eyes with my free hand.

"Are you alright?" she asked, voice gentle.

I started to give her the answer I gave everyone. *I'm perfectly well, thank you.* But that was a lie. I was not well. I was twisted up inside, somehow malformed and incomplete. Every doctor assured me that was not the case, but there must be something wrong with me. My body kept failing me, kept refusing to hold on to the one thing I wanted most.

"I had a miscarriage today," I said. Then I heard myself admit, "My thirteenth." Wasn't thirteen supposed to be a lucky number? Or was it unlucky?

Winona's hand convulsed around mine. "I—"

"Please don't say you're sorry," I blurted. I was so sick of hearing that. No one was more sorry than I was.

Winona was silent for a moment before she said, "I was going to say I cannot even imagine the pain you must be feeling."

"No," I whispered. My gaze went to her little girl. "You can't." I cleared my throat and pulled my hand free. "Well, I know it's early, but I think I need a drink."

I felt her gaze on me as I stood and crossed the kitchen to the refrigerator. I grabbed the bottle of expensive champagne I had bought when I reached the end of my first trimester. I had not opened it. I simply bought it to celebrate and was saving it until I could drink it after the baby came. I collected two flutes from the cabinet and returned to the table.

I manipulated the cork free, and Emma jumped at the loud pop. When I moved to pour Winona a glass, she placed her hand over the rim of the flute.

"I'm sorry, Joan." She met my gaze. "I can't drink right now."

I studied her. The evening sun pouring through the window gleamed against her skin. "You're pregnant," I said, and even I could hear the dullness in my voice.

She did not say anything for a long moment. "I am." An apology was in her tone.

I looked away and sat down heavily across from her. The unfairness of it all made my stomach churn. I skipped the glass and took a long gulp of champagne straight from the bottle. I thought again of how often my husband had slipped away in the middle of the night. I thought about the time I followed him and saw her slip into the front seat of his car.

"Is it Donald's?" I asked finally.

She leaned back as if I had shoved her. "*What?*" Disbelief was clear in her face and voice, but that could mean anything.

"I know you've been meeting my husband secretly for the last few months," I said.

She was silent for a moment. "I have been," she admitted, "but not for the reasons you are obviously thinking."

"Why, then? What reasons?"

She hesitated. "I can't tell you that, but I promise you, I have absolutely no interest in your husband in that way."

"Are you certain?" I asked. "Because your husband doesn't seem to have any interest in you."

Her face went blank, and she stared at me until I looked away. "I think we'll be going now." She pushed back from the table and tucked Emma on her hip. I stood as she did.

She paused beside me. "I am sorry for you, Joan,"

she said, and the pity in her voice as she stood there with a child in her arms and another growing inside her shattered my heart. It had been held together so tenuously already. I felt it crumble in my chest. "I know you must be in tremendous pain right now, and your anger must be great. So I'll let your comment pass."

I heard Donald's car pull into the drive.

"You don't need to give me a ride home," she said. "I'll get one from your husband."

I started to shake. The bottle of champagne was still clutched in my hand. It felt as if I stepped outside of myself as I turned and raised the heavy glass bottle. Champagne sluiced down my arm as I brought the bottle down as hard as I could on the back of Winona's head.

The bottle splintered in my hand.

Winona staggered at the top of the set of stairs leading down into the living room. I saw her arms lock around Emma for an instant before she went limp. She fell in what seemed like slow motion, and when I saw the direction her fall was taking it, I was the one who cried out.

I lunged for her, catching the back of her blouse in my hand, but her forward momentum ripped her away from me. When her temple hit the edge of the heavy cherry wood coffee table, the sound was violent and hollow, like a melon being burst by a blow.

She never made a sound. Emma, however, screamed hysterically.

I stumbled down the four steps and fell to my knees at her side.

"Oh god, oh god," I whispered.

Emma wailed, red faced and terrified. Already a knot was forming on her forehead where she had hit the floor. I carefully caught Winona's shoulder and rolled her to her back. She was limp, and the blood pouring from the deep, ugly wound in her head was bright.

I stripped off my cardigan and pressed it against her temple. The pink fabric was saturated far too quickly.

The car door slammed outside.

I pressed my fingers against Winona's throat and felt only stillness.

Footsteps rang on the front deck.

Emma continued to scream. I lifted her from the floor and cradled her in my arms. "It's okay, it's okay," I wept. She strained and struggled against me.

The front door opened, and my husband froze in the doorway. "What have you done?"

Twenty-Five

HECTOR

Ed was sleeping, but Betty's eyes opened as soon as I entered their shared room.

She studied me closely as I approached her bedside.

"Where is she?" she asked, voice low.

I glanced at Ed. The machines he was hooked to hummed quietly. He looked gaunt and colorless. Betty's eye was blackening in a bruise, and the bandage was livid against her head.

"Hector, where is she?" she asked again, gaze sharp on my face.

She did not need to clarify which *she*.

"She's gone," I admitted, and the words tasted like failure. "I don't know where she is. I've been searching but I can't find her anywhere."

I almost staggered under the weight of those words. I remembered how Winona had slammed the door behind her as she left, rattling the entire Airstream. I remembered how the days had turned into weeks, and then months, and then years. My girls had been there one moment and gone the next.

The not knowing where they were or what happened to them consumed me. It haunted my sleep. It tainted my food. The not knowing poisoned me. It had taken me several years before I realized it had driven me past the brink of sanity.

But living was a hard habit to break, so I got a dog to help me search for them and to give me a reason to drag myself out of bed every damn day.

Black spots danced before my eyes. I could not do it again. Not even Frank could help preserve my sanity if I could not find this girl who had forced her way into my life and had now disappeared. Just like the daughter she claimed to be.

I could not breathe. The air was trapped in my lungs, and my chest was caving in on itself.

A hand gripped mine, tight and anchoring. "In and out. In and out."

I followed the guidance until the darkness retreated from my vision and the vise around my chest loosened. Betty kept a tight hold on my hand, and I did not have the strength to pull away from her yet.

"She told me her sister was murdered in Denver," she said. My gaze flew to hers, but her eyes were closed, her brows pinched. "She didn't say what her sister's name was or give me any details. But she mentioned her sister was killed in a motel."

"Did she say when?" I asked.

Betty opened her eyes and shook her head. "Only that she felt responsible."

I needed to figure out what the files she had in her backpack were.

"I know she's not our Emma," Betty said quietly. "But—"

"But she's someone's Emma," I acknowledged.

"But I want you to look for her as if she were," Betty said.

She had always been a quiet woman, and she had never had much to say to me. "Do you still blame me?" I asked her now. I knew her husband did. I knew her son still did, even though we had reached a truce of sorts.

She held my gaze. "I blame whoever took them from us." I nodded and tried to draw my hand from her, but she clung to my fingers with surprising strength. "I thought it tragic that you never knew what you had until they were gone."

I swallowed, waiting for the anger and bitterness to pierce me. Neither did. I felt nothing but the hollowing emptiness of grief.

"I know now."

Too late, but neither of us said so aloud.

"It's not too late for this girl," Betty said, voice soft.

I did not promise I would find her. I knew how easily a promise like that was broken. I remained silent, but I nodded.

She finally relinquished her grip on my hand, but her voice caught me again when I reached the doorway of the hospital room.

"Do you remember what Winona did all those years?" I paused and looked back at her. "No matter what shift you worked at the police department."

I swallowed. I had not even recognized what Winona had done until I came home to a dark, empty trailer once she was gone. "She left a light on."

A bittersweet smile flitted across Betty's face. "I'll leave a light on for you."

"I need your help," I said as soon as he answered the phone.

"You got it," William Silva said before I could get another word in.

Maggie's son was retired Special Forces. He had done a short stint in the FBI and decided he preferred shades of gray to black and white. He had a wealth of resources and connections in addition to a sixth sense for finding people. It was why the sign on the door on his office in Denver said FUGITIVE RECOVERY AGENT.

He had been a solid kid, raised by strong, hard-working parents until his father had dropped dead of a heart attack at the age of forty-three. Then he had become a strong, hard-working son who helped his mother at the diner every day before and after school. He had only joined the military after he asked me to promise to look after his mother. He had been a good kid, but he was an even better man.

I filled him in on the girl who had shown up days ago claiming to be Emma.

He let out a low whistle. "Doesn't she know they'll have to do paternity tests?"

"I don't care about that," I said, and the truth of the words surprised me as much as the vehemence in my voice did. "She's missing."

Maggie, Evelyn, Jack, and I had spent hours searching for Annie yesterday and into the night. Frank traced her routes through town between the inn, diner, police department, and Ed and Betty's. He did not pick up on her scent anywhere else. She was gone without a trace.

And I knew, deep in my gut, something was wrong. It was the same gnawing edge I felt when Donald Marsden showed up on my doorstep fifteen years ago and told me Winona's car had been found abandoned on the side of the road, but there was no trace of my girls.

I sat at the table in the kitchen of the inn and laid the files in Annie's backpack out in front of me. Each file was for a separate individual. They all appeared to be medical records, but there was one striking similarity that grabbed me by the throat. All of the records were for girls, most of them still in their teens, though a few were in their twenties or thirties. The average age was fifteen. Some had their race marked as *white*. The majority were black, Latina, or American Indian.

Unease gripped me.

The files all had the same letterhead listing an address in Cherry Hills Village, a community south of Denver.

"I'm coming to Denver," I said. "I need you to do some digging on a possible murder that took place there."

"Where and when?"

"I don't know. I'm guessing within the last month. Female victim, possibly found in a motel room in Denver. Native American, but I don't know her age. I'm assuming young, teens or twenties."

"That's not much to go on," he said. "But I'll see what I can find. I'll start with the Jane Does from the last three months."

"I'll be there tomorrow. I'll call you when I'm getting into town. There's a place I want to check out in Cherry Hills Village."

"Send me the address," William said. "I'll meet you there."

I hung up the phone and strode down the hall to my small apartment in the back corner of the inn. Frank trotted at my heels and took up a sprawl on the bed to watch curiously as I packed a duffel bag. His tail began to thump as I packed food for him as well.

When I returned to the kitchen, Evelyn stood at the table flipping through the files.

She glanced up when I entered the room and pushed her glasses up from where they had slid down her nose. "Who are these women?" she asked.

Victims, I thought, but I was not certain how. "I don't know," I said. "But I'm going to find out."

Her eyes moved between my duffel and the letterhead on the files. "You're going to Colorado," she guessed.

I nodded. She moved aside as I collected the files and placed them back in Annie's backpack.

"Do you think you'll find her there?"

"It's the only clue I have to go on about why she showed up here in the first place," I said. I knew Maggie had told her the truth about the girl's identity.

"I'll keep searching here in town while you're gone," Evelyn said. "I know Maggie and others will as well."

I stopped as I slung the backpack over my shoulder. I had used the woman who stood before me. She had been nothing more than a pawn to me, a woman I had hoped would bait the man I spent fifteen years believing was responsible for Winona and Emma's disappearance. My sacrificial lamb, as William had called her once.

I had never allowed myself to feel guilt about the role I played in her close call with a serial killer, but as I studied her now, I felt the burn of remorse in my chest. Regardless of what I suspected had happened to her stalker years ago, she had been an innocent victim caught in my need for vengeance. She was flesh and blood. She could be damaged and wounded, even killed. She was someone's daughter.

"I'm sorry."

I was not certain who was more startled by my words.

Her brows arched and then lowered. "For what?"

For being willing to let you die just so I could catch a killer. It was little better than killing her myself and framing Jeff Roosevelt for the crime.

"For leaving you to deal with the guests," I said.

She studied me, eyes the color of a single malt, a knowing in her gaze that said she knew I had not meant my apology for that. "You always do that anyway," she said. There was a smile in her voice, though, no heat.

"You do a good job," I said.

She laughed. "Well, at least a better one than you." Her laugh trailed away. "Keep us posted. We'll keep looking."

Jack's truck was parked at the end of the drive. I let my truck idle as he approached with a bag over his shoulder.

"Hop in the backseat," I told Frank as Jack rounded the truck and headed to the passenger's side.

"I'm coming with you," Jack said as he opened the door and slid into the passenger's seat.

"I don't think we're to the point of being friendly enough to road trip together," I said, though I put my truck in gear and left the inn's drive.

The other man huffed out a breath and flipped me off as he settled low in the seat. He leaned his head back against the seat and was asleep before we made it to Gardiner. He was snoring softly by the time I passed Livingston.

Once I passed Big Timber, the mountains faded into the haze in the rearview mirror. The land was wide and flat, the road featureless and unending.

I did not drive east too often. Away from the mountains, the land reminded me uncomfortably of the place where I had been born and left to raise myself. Windswept and empty, swallowed up by the sky. Forgotten middle America where the people perpetually squinted against the sun and lived and died within a narrow radius of plains. The endless openness had always left a knot in my throat. I had never been out on a boat in the ocean before, but I imagined that featureless stretch of barrenness was just as haunting.

Places like this whittled people down to bone and sinew and bitterness. My mother had been a prime example.

I had a clear memory of playing in the dirt along the side of a deserted road as a boy. The car we were living in had broken down. No one had passed us on the road for two days.

My mother sat on the hood of the car. The engine had finally stopped smoking the previous day. Where she had gotten the bottle of whiskey, I did not know. There always seemed to be one attached to her hand. A cigarette clung to her lips.

I thought I must have been around five years old. The dirt was as dry and scabbed as rust, but I found a flower in the blade-like grass. It was probably a weed, spindly and scraggly and stubbornly clinging to life the way weeds do. I remembered the small flower that capped the weed was yellow.

I ran to where my mother lounged on the hood and offered her the flower. Her face never moved as she studied it.

"I picked a flower for you," I said when she made no move to take it.

"It'll be dead soon," she said, voice as dry and distant as the sky. "You've killed it."

The flower looked so small, and it had tried so hard to live in that thirsty dirt. I tried to put it back in the ground, but it looked sad and limp by the time I finished replanting it. I had nothing to water it with save the tears that dripped off my chin.

"Stop sniveling, boy," my mother called.

If she had ever given me a name, I never knew it. I only ever heard her say *boy* or *bastard*. It was not until I went to school one day at the age of nine and told the teacher my name was *Boy* that I realized what I was missing. The teacher had been pretty, always smiling, and her hands were soft. I immediately wished she was my mother.

She gently told me I was a boy, but that was not my

name. I had been stumped. I glanced around the room and heard the whispers and giggles. My ears grew hot. My gaze landed on another boy in class. He was the tallest boy in the room. His hair was dark, and when another boy had laughed at his accent and the dirt on his clothes, he had punched him in the nose. I wanted to be like that boy.

"My name is Hector," I said, borrowing the other boy's name.

But there in the dirt by the side of the road, I was still just *boy*.

"I didn't mean to kill it," I whispered, gulping back the rest of my tears.

My mother laughed, and it was a mean sound. "No need to cry over it. Look around you. Nothing survives here. These are killing fields."

The term made me shiver. Suddenly, the grass no longer seemed like dry blades but like slivers of bones jutting up from their grave.

Killing fields. I had to fight the urge to shudder now as I drove, accompanied by a snoring man who had once been my enemy and my snoring poodle.

Night had fallen by the time I reached Billings. The darkness hid the open expanse of the land. Forty-five minutes east of Billings, the interstate curved south and veered through the Crow Reservation. An hour later, I crossed the Wyoming state line.

I had been driving for five hours when I pulled over at a widening in the road that claimed to be the town of Kaycee. I let Frank out of the cab to stretch his legs and do his business while I filled the truck's tank with diesel.

Jack stirred when I opened the door and grabbed Frank's bowl and a bottle of water.

He stretched and scrubbed a hand over his face. "Let me get a cup of coffee, and I'll drive the rest of the way."

I did not argue with him. I shared the bottle of water with Frank and then took up my post in the passenger's seat as Jack got behind the wheel. Frank curled up in the backseat. I leaned my seat back and closed my eyes.

The motion of the road rocked me, but sleep eluded me. The oncoming headlights on the highway were a flashing strobe against my eyelids. I thought about all the times I had called a car home when I was a boy. I thought about the girl who had come to me for help, and I only acknowledged her once she lied to me about being my daughter.

The sun gleamed in varying shades of pink and purple on the towering summit of Long's Peak as we reached the far edge of Denver's suburban sprawl. Even in the middle of August, snow capped the dramatic peaks of the Rockies west of the city.

Jack pulled off the highway at the Westminster exit and paid for the next tank of diesel. We traded off driving again.

"Look in the backpack," I said, nodding to the backseat, "and get me directions for the address listed on those files."

While he did so, I called William. It was early, but he answered on the second ring.

"We just reached Denver," I said.

"We?" William asked.

"Jack's with me."

He was quiet on the other end of the line for a beat. "You trust that wily motherfucker?"

Jack had roughly a decade on William, and the two

men had never been friends. I glanced at my brother-in-law from the corner of my eye.

"Until he proves that I can't," I said.

Jack snorted.

"Good enough," William said. "I'll meet you at the address. I've found something."

"We'll be there in forty."

I expected an office or a warehouse, but the GPS on the phone led me to a home in one of the wealthiest neighborhoods in America. Or what remained of a home.

I left the engine running with the air conditioner on high for Frank and exited the truck. The slam of the passenger door indicated Jack followed me.

I stood on the sidewalk and took in the destruction. Fire had ravaged the house and destroyed it almost down to the foundation. This was not a neighborhood with houses clustered together in suburban congestion. There was immaculate lawn stretched around the destruction, containing the damage to the burnt husk of a house.

"What the hell happened here?" Jack asked, coming to stand beside me.

I heard a car pull up to the curb and turned to find William Silva striding toward us.

He was not an overly tall man. He stood several inches under six feet, and he shared his mother's wiry frame. He did not look like a formidable man. In fact, he looked like he would be more apt to do your taxes. But if I had to choose a man to watch my back in dangerous circumstances, William would be my first choice every time.

"Arson," he said when he reached us. "I read the investigator's report. Happened a week ago. There was so much accelerant used firefighters didn't have a hope of putting it out."

"Anyone killed?"

"House was empty. As in, bare."

I frowned. "Unoccupied?"

"Not according to neighbors," William said. "Someone lived here, but hours before the blaze starting, neighbors said they saw moving vans at the house."

"What do the housing records say?" Jack asked.

"That's where things get interesting. I did some digging. The house is owned by a corporation."

"Which one?" I asked.

"One that doesn't exist," William said. "And the night before the fire, someone called the police. Said she thought she saw someone lurking around the house, possibly a B and E. But when the police showed up, whoever met the officers at the door turned them away and said it was a false alarm."

I rubbed my jaw, studying the warped wreckage of the sprawling house.

"You think the girl set the fire?" Jack asked.

"No," I said. "I'm thinking the fire was to erase evidence of whoever was living here. I think she was the burglar and what she took was enough to send them running to ground."

Twenty-Six

Joan

now

I hit Emma too hard. I meant to simply stun her, but the figurine I had lifted from the table in the entryway was heavy and I put more force behind the swing than I intended.

The sound she made when she hit the floor was the same one her mother had. A heavy thud that sounded strangely hollow and made me flinch. For an instant, I thought I was staring down at Winona again.

Blood was not pooling beneath Emma's face, though. When I carefully turned her over, blood streaked down her cheek and matted the hair at her temple, but it was nowhere near the amount of blood that had flooded my floor when Winona fell.

The knot growing on Emma's head looked angry and painful. I left her where she was sprawled and moved into the kitchen to grab an ice pack. I had an assortment of them. After fifteen years, I was an expert in reducing swelling and bruising.

I knelt beside her and eased her head into my lap. She moaned when I pressed the ice pack against her head. The knot was the size of a golf ball now. I stroked her hair back from her face.

I did not know how she had done it, how she was back after all these years. She had to remember what had happened. She had to recall what I had done.

Donald would kill me over this.

I glanced at my watch. He would be home in an hour or so. The meeting with the sheriff's department, other police departments, and the fire stations throughout the county had begun at seven at the park headquarters in Yellowstone. This was the worst wildfire season the national park had seen since 1988. Uncertainty was as thick as the smoke in the air.

I put the ice pack back in the freezer and then dragged Emma down the hall to the door leading to the cellar. She was heavily and limp, and aside from another moan, she did not even stir.

I hated going down into the cellar. Fifteen years ago, a week after it happened, I had moved everything from the unused nursery into the cellar. I had threatened to never go down the stairs again unless Donald built a room so I did not have to see everything I had collected over the years. I wanted that old dream closed off and locked away in the dark.

The laundry room was downstairs, and since Donald wanted to wear clean, pressed shirts every day, he built the room in the far corner of the cellar.

After he had become chief a few years ago, he had not had time to use his workshop. He would not be going down into the cellar over the next few days.

I backed down the steep steps slowly, arms wrapped around Emma from behind, her head hanging against my chest. Her heels bounced down each step. I noticed that the laces were untied on one of her sneakers. When we reached the bottom of the steps, I knelt and tied her shoe before dragging her across the cold cement floor to the room Donald had built.

I had insisted on a padlock for the door. I did not want to be tempted to go inside and sit amongst my dead dream. Donald sighed but he had complied with my wishes and hidden the key.

What he did not know was that one day I had turned the cellar upside down until I found the key hidden at the bottom of a jar of bolts. I had never unlocked the door, but some days, it was a comfort to simply stand at the door and hold the key.

I held my breath as I unlocked the door. As I opened the door, the air escaped on a sigh of dust and longing. This was a dark corner of the cellar, and Donald had not bothered with wiring the room for a light switch or its own light.

I was thankful for the dark. I knew each item in this room, but I did not want to see the entire collection sitting forlornly in the deep shadows collecting dust and spiders.

I dragged Emma inside, and then I forced myself to turn my back, close the door, and snap the padlock into place. I leaned my forehead against the door.

I needed to know what she remembered and why she had come back. Surely it was for more than simply to haunt me.

There was a smear of blood on my blouse, I realized.

I unbuttoned it as I moved back to Donald's workshop area and deposited the key back at the bottom of the jar of bolts. I placed the jar back on the shelf and moved to the washing machine.

Once I had a load in the wash, including my stained blouse, I donned a dirty, wrinkled shirt from the pile of laundry that still needed to be done and climbed the stairs. My body felt heavy and drained. I wandered down the hall back to the front entry.

I picked up the heavy figurine from where I had dropped it on the floor. It was a beautiful piece of sculpture depicting a wolf mother and her pup. There was blood on the wolf mother's back from where I had struck Emma. I wiped it away.

I placed the sculpture back on the table and looked at the floor. The woven rug in the entryway had a small stain on it as well. When I dampened a cloth in the kitchen and blotted the spot, it seemed to fade into the pattern of the rug.

I rinsed the cloth at the sink and draped it over the counter to dry before taking a seat at the kitchen table. My hands trembled.

I had known this day would come. I just had not expected my reckoning to come in the form of the very child I had killed.

Twenty-Seven

HECTOR

now

We migrated to a tavern near William's office that opened early. The patio was dog-friendly, and after we ordered food, the waitress brought Frank a bowl full of water and a bone.

Even here, miles away from Yellowstone, the sky was hazy and the scent of smoke hung in the air, stirred by the fans overhead.

While we waited for our food to arrive, William told us what he had discovered.

"There have been two Jane Does found in Denver in the last few weeks," he said. "One was black. The other was listed as white in the case report, but I got the pictures from the autopsy. I think she was American Indian."

"What happened to her?" I asked.

"A maid at a nearby motel found her when they went in to clean the room. Poor kid was strangled to death."

"Is Denver PD investigating it?"

William grimaced. "You know how it is. They list the case as active, but no one came forward to claim her. Plenty of fingerprint hits in AFIS from those lifted from the hotel room, but none matching the girl's. They followed up with the other hits, but they were dead ends. They chalked it up to a prostitute killed by a john. Or…" He took a drink and rubbed his chin.

"Or what?" Jack asked.

"There was something else. I read the autopsy report. The kid was early teens. Best guess was twelve to fourteen. She was pregnant."

"Maybe someone wasn't interested in being a father," Jack said.

I glanced out at the quiet street. The wheels were turning in my head. "She doesn't fit any missing persons report?"

"No," William said. "I double checked that myself. No ID on her or in the motel room anywhere. Her DNA isn't in the system. The only identifier was a butterfly tattoo on her hip."

Jack's head came up. "A butterfly?"

"Yeah," William said.

He turned to me. "Let me see the files you brought."

I handed him the backpack and watched him closely as he flipped through the files until he finally found what he was looking for. "I'm thinking this girl is probably your Jane Doe."

He handed me the file for Kimimela Between Lodges.

"How do you know?" William asked.

"Because Kimimela means *butterfly*."

I paged through her file. She was one of the half dozen I had noted who was from the Pine Ridge Reservation. Her home was listed as Allen, South Dakota. She was twelve years old.

The file listed her height and a chart of her weight over a five-month period. There were extensive notes about her personality, about her emotional state of mind, about her level of intelligence. Her health history was described in detail, down to the time she fell out of a tree and broke her arm at the age of six. Sexual history and menstrual history were covered, and her physical characteristics were covered in minute detail. Her bone structure, complexion, tanning ability, eye color and set, hair color and type.

Family and genetic history were covered. I noticed gaps in the information the girl had provided. She listed no information for her father or for his side of the family.

The notes went on for forty pages. There were questionnaires throughout that the girl had painstakingly filled out. Her handwriting was young and full of loops and bubbles and misspellings. She was asked to list favorite books and movies, what inspired and motivated her, what her hopes and dreams were. She wrote in the margins, print shrinking as she ran out of space.

I could only think of two reasons for a questionnaire this detailed, and neither option set well with me.

The waitress placed our food in front of us. I had been hungry, but the implications of a dossier this detailed turned my stomach.

"Where do you go from here?" William asked, watching me closely.

I glanced at Jack. "We need to go to Pine Ridge."

William gave us the spare key to his house. "While you head to South Dakota, I'll go to Raven's Gap and search for the kid."

"If you find anything—"

He clasped my shoulder. "You'll be the first to know. Rest before you head out again. You look like shit."

Jack took William's spare bedroom. Frank claimed the couch in the living room, and I kicked back in the recliner. I slept in snatches for a few hours. At noon, we headed north.

When Jack took the wheel, I distracted myself from the emptiness of Nebraska and pulled up a search for Pine Ridge on my phone's internet browser. Reception was spotty, but it was enough to load several pages for me to read.

Pine Ridge Indian Reservation was located in the southwest corner of South Dakota. It was the seventh largest reservation in the country. It was also the poorest. The average life expectancy was in the mid-sixties. Oglala Lakota County was the poorest county in the nation with a per capita income of less than ten thousand dollars.

The unemployment rate was at almost ninety percent, and over half of the inhabitants of the reservation lived below the poverty rate. High school dropout rates were over seventy percent. Allen, South Dakota, our destination, was ranked as the poorest community in America.

Even with that knowledge, nothing prepared me.

Most of the streets were empty and unpaved. The

few buildings were depressed and weathered. Rusted cars were abandoned in overgrown lots in front of homes sinking on their foundations. *A-town* was a garish, spray-painted tattoo across most of the buildings.

There was no internet service, and there was no address listed in Kimimela Between Lodges's file, only the name of the town.

The door was propped open to a wooden building painted red situated right alongside the street. I pulled to the side of the empty road.

"I'll go in and ask for directions," Jack said. When I moved to turn the truck off, he continued, "Don't come in with me. You do, they won't tell me anything."

I sat in the truck and waited as he disappeared inside. Frank whined in the backseat. A thin dog wandered across the street in front of us, highlighted by the setting sun. I reached back and rubbed Frank's ears.

Jack trotted across the street toward us and leapt back into the passenger's seat. "Head east down the next road," he said.

A few miles later, he pointed out a turnoff to the left.

The drive was a rough, rutted path, and I kept my truck at a crawl. The trail leading to my property outside of Raven's Gap was smoother than this path, even after the wear of winter. Jack braced a hand against the roof of the truck.

It was a half mile before I spotted it. My stomach tightened as I drove closer. I parked and stared.

"Fuck," Jack breathed.

It could not even be called a house. It was a decrepit structure consisting of little more than an old camper patched up with scrap wood and tarps.

"Fuck," Jack said again. "How long have those girls lived here?"

I did not have an answer for him. I had known poverty once, but I was a long time removed from it. The memory of that desperation, isolation, and tattered pride felt like a punch in the gut.

A battered, rusted car was parked beside the camper. The hood was propped open, and a bundle of wires connected the car's battery to a generator by the sagging front door. Twenty-five yards past the decrepit camper, a shack listed on its foundations. I had a feeling it served as an outhouse.

I got out of the truck. Frank moved to leap to the ground, but I put a hand out to prevent him from following me. "Stay in the truck," I told him, and closed the door.

A voice suddenly shouted at me from within the trailer, but I did not understand any of the words.

I stopped and glanced back to see Jack getting out of the truck.

"I'm not here looking for trouble," I called.

When the response came, I looked to Jack for translation.

"He said this is his home now and he has every right to be here," Jack said.

"Tell him I'm looking for information about the family that used to live here," I said, but before Jack could repeat what I had said, a response was shouted from inside.

I glanced at Jack when he remained silent for a long moment. He scowled. "He said the girls aren't here any longer, and he didn't have anything to do with the dead body."

"Whose dead body?" I called to the man inside the camper, who could obviously understand me but only responded in Lakota.

"The one in the bedroom," Jack said after listening to the response from inside.

I started toward the front door, but a tarp that served as a window edged aside. I saw the shotgun barrel at the same time I heard the blasting report of it being fired.

"Shit!" Jack said, ducking back behind my truck. He scrambled to the passenger's side door and disappeared inside.

The shot had gone wide, missing me to kick up shards of dirt and scrubby clots of grass ten feet to my left. Frank barked wildly from the cab of the truck.

It was just a warning shot, but I heeded the warning and backed away until I opened my door and climbed back in my truck.

In truth, I was relieved. I had not wanted to see the inside of that dilapidated hovel. I had not wanted to imagine that young girl with her serious, earnest face and hopeful eyes living in such poverty.

As soon as she claimed she was Emma, I had assumed she had no parents, no one searching for her. Now I wondered how long she had been left to fend for herself.

The sun had set by the time we reached that same red wooden building again. I braked in front of it.

"Go ask them where the sheriff's department is," I ordered.

The directions Jack received took us south of Allen

to a T in the road. I turned left and nine miles later we reached the slightly less depressed widening of the road of Martin, South Dakota.

The Bennett County Sheriff's Office was a long rectangular building made of brick, windowless and featureless.

A young woman was sitting behind a glass partition. She looked up when I approached.

"I want to talk to someone about the Between Lodges family. They live outside of Allen," I said. I remembered the words Jack had translated. "A body was found there recently."

It was the sheriff himself who came out into the postage stamp sized lobby a few minutes later.

"Benjamin Looking Horse," he said, extending his hand.

He had at least a decade on me, and I had a foot of height on him. His handshake was firm, though.

After Jack and I introduced ourselves, he gestured for us to follow him. "Come on back to my office." His office was as sterile and featureless as the rest of the building. "Kayley said you had questions about the Between Lodges."

"I'm looking for Annie," I said. "Kimimela was her younger sister? Does she have any other siblings?"

"Just the two of them, as far as I know. Annie's the older sister by four years." The sheriff sighed. "I didn't even know the girls were gone and the house was abandoned until Jimmy came in here babbling one night."

"Jimmy?"

"Jimmy Bison Eater. The resident drunk." He grimaced. "Or the drunk I scrape off the side of the road most often."

"I think we met him tonight at their…" I hesitated to even call it a house. "At their camper."

"He's still squatting there? I pick my battles."

"He told us he had nothing to do with the dead body," I said. "What dead body?"

"Same thing he told me when he stumbled in here drunk one night. I thought it was just the alcohol talking, but I went and checked it out." He rubbed a hand over his face. "The community failed those girls. I don't have an excuse for it. They were both good kids. The older one especially. Always picking up odd jobs, hardworking, always looking out for her little sister. Hell, Annie raised Kimi. The younger one was a good kid, too. Just…wild. Not a troublemaker. Just too pretty and smart for her own good. Always getting into mischief if her sister turned her back on her for a minute. The last couple years she'd started hanging out with a bad crowd."

"What about their parents?" Jack asked.

"Who can say about their father. I would guess someone local, but no one ever stepped up to claim them after their mother went missing."

The words were like a punch to the gut. "What happened to her?" I asked.

The chief of police glanced at Jack. "You know how it is out here. Women gone in an instant, and we're lucky if we find their bodies. Their mother left to get medicine one night when the littlest one was sick. She made it to the store here in Martin around four in the morning. The clerk remembered her. She never made it home."

"Did anyone look after them?" Jack asked.

The chief nodded. "Their mother's grandmother. She was old and in poor health ten years ago, and everyone thought she was homebound at this point. That's what Annie told everyone."

"The grandmother was the dead body in the house," I guessed.

The chief looked away and swore under his breath. "She'd been dead for years. No foul play. She died of old age. She had diabetes, and the coroner said it looked like kidney failure from what he could tell at this point. She was practically mummified in the only bed in that camper. I can only imagine what those girls went through, why they decided not to tell anyone." He turned his gaze back to me. "You said you're looking for Annie? What about Kimi?"

"Kimi was found in a motel in Denver last week," I said. "She was strangled to death."

"Shit," he breathed.

"Annie went missing Saturday night from Raven's Gap, Montana. I think her disappearance is linked to Kimi's murder."

"After we found the girls' grandmother, I started asking around," he said. "Something I should've done months ago. Years ago."

I did not tell the man that he could not have known what was going on. I knew how heavy that burden of responsibility felt after a tragedy.

"Rumor around school was Kimi had started partying with some of the boys in the local gang. The booze flows freely at those bonfires they have."

"She was twelve," I pointed out.

The chief sliced me with a look. "You think there's much for a kid to do here on the rez? This isn't suburban America with your little league sports and your book clubs."

I raised my hands, conceding his point.

"I don't know how many of the pregnancies that have happened since the gangs got so prevalent have been the result of rape. The women here don't talk about these things. At least not to me." Bitterness twisted his features. "They figure why bother. But I know the clinic has been getting a lot of business in the last few years."

"The autopsy said Kimimela was pregnant," I said. I had been weighing two options after studying Kimimela Between Lodges's file. That stack of files in the backpack in my truck started leaning one direction.

"Then the rumors at school were true," the chief said. "She dropped out of school and was gone."

"Gone where?"

"No one knew, and her sister wasn't talking."

"What about the clinic you mentioned?" Jack asked.

"It's up in Kyle," he said. "Only decent, modern facility we have access to in the area, unless you want to go to the hospital in Pine Ridge. It's run by a white woman, though, so not many are willing to go see her."

"Except for women who need help," I said.

He eyed me carefully. "There's a lot that goes on here that you could not even fathom. Poverty like you would not believe. There are not a lot of options for my people. She gives women, girls, a choice, and I'm not willing to see you take that away from them, if you're thinking of causing trouble for her."

"I'm not looking to bring a malpractice suit against her," I told him. "Or to turn her in. All I care about is finding Annie."

He nodded. "Then if you're looking for answers, she might be able to give you some."

Twenty-Eight

Joan

then

"What the fuck have you done?" Donald repeated. He closed the front door behind him and locked it quickly.

I staggered to my feet, struggling to hold on to Emma as she strained against me. Her face was damp and red as she screamed and wailed.

"I—I don't know," I whispered.

His gaze dropped to Winona, limp on the floor at my feet. "You don't know?" He crossed the room and knelt beside her. His fingers went to her throat and then he clasped her wrist, brow drawn in concentration. After a long moment, he placed her arm over her stomach and stood slowly. He stared at me as if he had never seen me before. "She's dead."

A sob burst from my throat. I shifted Emma on my hip, and I started to lift my hand to my mouth. I froze at the sight of Winona's blood staining my hand. "I didn't—I didn't mean it. I didn't mean to!"

"You need to tell me exactly what happened."

I did, and he paced back and forth through the living room. His face never changed, even when I told him about my trip to the hospital.

When I finished, he said, "I told you not to get your hopes up."

I sat down heavily on the sofa. I clutched Emma to me. Her screaming had finally abated, and she rested against my chest. Her damp, hot faced was buried in my neck, and her breath rasped in her throat.

"Were you sleeping with her?" I asked.

"No," he said shortly. "She came to me with evidence she found about Larson."

"Larson?"

"Grant Larson. He owns the Broken Arrow. And apparently he runs a poaching operation on the side." He raked a hand through his hair. "This was going to be big, Joan. Huge. It would have guaranteed I made chief. And now..." He gestured toward the woman lying dead in our living room floor.

I could not look at her. "What do we do? We need to call the station."

"Don't be an idiot," he snapped. I jumped at the crack in his tone, and Emma lurched against me. "Do you know how this would look? I'm supposed to make commander next year. Do you think I'll still get that, still have a chance to be chief if my fucking wife is a murderer?"

I flinched.

"Jesus," he whispered. "You've ruined everything, and for absolutely nothing."

I pressed my lips together and rubbed a hand

against Emma's back when she whimpered. "What are we going to do?" I whispered.

"Did anyone see you pick her up on the side of the road?"

"No," I said.

"What about when you were coming to the house? Anyone pass you who would have seen her in your car?"

"No, there was no one." I swallowed. "What are we going to do?" I asked again.

"We're going to take care of it." He stared down at Winona and rubbed a hand wearily along his jaw. "Christ. I'm going to change out of my uniform. We'll wait until it's dark."

I was on edge, horror and fear locking my throat tight.

Once his police uniform was in the hamper in the laundry room and he had changed, Donald went out into the garage and came back with a tarp.

I had been frozen on the couch, staring at the soles of Winona's boots. I stood to leave the room. I couldn't watch.

"Sit," Donald said. "Sit there and watch. This is your doing."

He wrapped her in the plastic tarp neatly and tightly and then secured the tarp with duct tape. Emma leaned against my hold, arms outstretched toward her mother. I turned her away from the scene and pressed her cheek to my chest, holding her tight even as she struggled and protested.

He grunted as he lifted Winona's body in his arms. "Get ready," he said. "We'll take the truck."

My knees felt liquid, and I stumbled to the bedroom I had long ago converted into a nursery. It was unused but filled with years of hope and heartache. I retrieved the car seat I had purchased. It was one that converted into a baby carrier. Emma was too big for it, but it would have to do.

I closed my eyes as Donald drove. My stomach churned sourly. I felt the moment we went off road, but I did not open my eyes. I rocked and swayed with the movement of the truck and wished with every fiber of my being that I could start the day anew. Perhaps this was all just a nightmare and I would wake up from it any moment.

It seemed like hours later when the truck lurched to a halt. I opened my eyes, but I could see nothing in the darkness.

"Where are we?" I whispered.

"Carry the flashlight," Donald said. "And bring Emma in the car seat."

The little girl had fallen into a fitful, exhausted sleep. The baby carrier was heavy and awkward, and it would leave a bruise from thumping against my hip. My shoulder burned with the weight of carrying her, and the beam of light I carried bobbed unsteadily.

We were deep in the mountains, the woods dense and black around us. We walked for over a mile.

"It's around here somewhere," Donald said, voice hushed. Winona, bound tightly in plastic, was draped over his shoulder.

I did not ask what he was looking for, and when he found the opening to the mine shaft, I did not ask how he had known it was here.

"I don't want to go in there," I whispered, staring at the gaping mouth leading into deeper darkness.

He turned suddenly and grabbed my face. I lurched in shock, dropping the flashlight. His fingers bit into my cheeks, and his thumb dug into my jaw.

"And I don't want to have a murderer for a wife," he said, and his breath was hot on my face. He let me go as quickly as he had grabbed me, and I staggered. "Lead the way and watch for drop-offs. I remember one about a hundred yards down the shaft."

I was shaking as I bent to grab the flashlight. I could still feel the impression of his fingers on my skin. Donald had a temper, but he only raised his voice in anger. He had never once, not in our twelve years of marriage, raised a hand to me.

The mine shaft was the stuff of nightmares. The smell was dank and loamy. The darkness was almost impenetrable. In places, parts of the roof had collapsed. My light fell upon rock piles from the walls sliding in on one another and wooden poles lodged to support the precarious beams overhead. Bones littered the floor.

"Please, Donald."

"Keep going," he said behind me, breathing labored. "It's not far."

The drop-off yawned out of the darkness, and I stopped, too frightened to move closer. The entire shaft seemed one breath away from collapsing.

I gently placed the baby carrier on the ground and rolled my shoulder to ease the burning ache.

"It's there," I whispered.

I turned away when Donald moved past me, but I heard his grunt followed by a long moment of silence before a deep, hollow thump reverberated through the shaft. I thought I would be sick.

I fought not to flinch when his hand landed on my shoulder. When I bent to pick up the baby carrier, his hand tightened.

"Leave her as well."

"No." Horror sliced through me. "No, Donald, *no*."

His fingers would leave bruises on my shoulder.

"How exactly do you think you would explain this?" he snapped.

The brevity of what I had done was like a blow to the stomach. I staggered. "Please," I said, and my words were choked, strangled by tears. "Please don't do this." I wept brokenly. "We can't do this!"

The blow seemed to come out of nowhere. His hand cracked across my cheekbone so hard a flash of white burst across my vision. I stumbled backward, tripped over the baby carrier, and fell hard in the dirt. The flashlight rolled away, spinning light over this nightmarish place.

A shower of debris from the ceiling rained down on my head.

Donald jerked me to my feet so quickly my neck cracked. "Listen to me, Joan." He shook me roughly. "Do you want to go to prison?"

A sob felt like it cracked my chest open.

"*We* haven't done anything," he said. "You did. You did this. I'm just trying to protect you."

Falling over her had awakened Emma, and she cried now. Her voice was small and plaintive and confused in the darkness.

I shrugged out of Donald's grip and knelt beside

the little girl. She was strapped into the baby carrier. Her arms and legs kicked against the restraints. I had tucked a blanket I had knit several weeks ago around her, but her movements now had knocked it loose.

"Shh," I whispered. I stroked a hand over her cheek. "Shh, darling."

She sniffed. "Mama?" Her voice was an uncertain warble.

I brushed her hair back from her forehead. "Mama's here with you. Shh now."

I tucked the blanket around her and hummed the lullaby I had learned for all the babies I could not have. When she drew in a shuddering breath, I began to sing, and the hollowness of the sound in the bowels of the earth sounded more like a dirge than a comfort.

She relaxed slowly, and then in the way of children, her lashes fell against her cheek and she was asleep. I let my song taper off to a whisper.

I studied her in the dim glow of the flashlight. The dark curls, the long lashes, the rounded baby cheeks. I let one finger ghost across her forehead, down her small snub of a nose. Her lips parted in sleep, and I touched the dimple in her chin.

I had prayed for so many years for a miracle, for this one gift. I had begged and pleaded. No more, I decided. There would be no more trying. There would be no more hope. What I had done—what I was about to do—was unforgivable. God had not answered my prayers for the last twelve years. He certainly would not now. He would not forget this. Nor would I.

I leaned over Emma and pressed my lips to her head. I paused and breathed in that sweet smell all young children carried with them.

Donald snagged my flashlight and my arm. He dragged me away.

"Please," I whispered. A sob was caught in my chest. "*Please.*"

He did not stop.

Twenty-Nine

HECTOR

The Crossroads Inn had two vacant rooms and no issues with Frank staying in my room. I surprised myself by falling into a deep sleep despite the yelling from the room next door.

The next morning as we passed through Allen again, Jack said, “Let me out here.”

With no sight of the skinny dog from yesterday lurking around, there was even less traffic on the road today. I stopped in the middle of the street.

“I want to ask around, see if anyone remembers anything they wouldn’t have told the sheriff,” he said.

I nodded. “I’ll be back through in a few hours.”

He nodded toward the opposite side of the road where the red wooden building was perched on the shoulder. “I’ll meet you there.”

Kyle was a twenty-minute drive to the northwest of Allen. The sheriff had given me directions to the clinic, and I was surprised to find my destination was a house.

It was the same blocky construction as the other houses in the area, but there were window boxes filled with flowers and the exterior either had a fresh coat of paint or had been power washed free of dirt recently.

A sign by the front door invited me to enter, and the small emblem in the bottom corner of the front window caught my eye as I opened the door. A bell chimed, announcing my entry, and after a moment, a woman appeared in the hallway and approached me.

"Good afternoon." She glanced at Frank at my side. "He's lovely, but I don't usually allow animals inside."

"He's a service dog," I lied.

I could not tell if she believed me or not, but she did not question his nonexistent certification.

"How may I help you?" she asked.

I glanced around. The place was clean, but it looked more like someone's living room than a waiting area. "This is the doctor's office?" I asked.

Her smile was tired but genuine. "Yes, but run by a woman who isn't a doctor," she admitted. She was white, and her accent told me she was a long way from home. I would guess home was somewhere on the east coast.

"Nurse practitioner?" I guessed.

"Guilty." She extended a hand. "Kay Overton."

I shook her hand. "Hector. I'm hoping you can tell me about a young girl who may have visited your office."

Her smile remained in place, but it lost its charm and became sharply polite. "I'm sorry, but I'm not allowed to discuss my patients."

"What if your patient was found dead in a hotel in Denver?"

The politeness fell away to shock as she paled.

"Who?"

"Kimimela Between Lodges," I said, watching her face.

The flinch was almost imperceptible, but it was there. "Why don't you come into my office?"

Frank trotted at my heels as she led me down the hall and into a sunny room that was far from a sterile doctor's office. She caught me taking in the room.

"My patients are usually uncomfortable about coming to see me. Not just because I'm a white outsider. I try to make this clinic as welcoming and comfortable as possible. Like they were coming to my home."

She took a seat in one of the chairs while I settled on the couch across from her. Frank crossed to her side, and I was surprised when she smiled at him and immediately began petting him.

"Why did Kimimela come to you?" I asked. She looked away. "Look," I said. "I'm not the authorities. I'm not going to report you."

Her gaze came back to me, and the twist to her lips was bitter. "Mr. Hector—"

"Just Hector."

"Hector," she said, "do you have any idea the war that is taking place against women in this country right now?"

"No," I admitted.

She leaned toward me. "Rich old white men in Washington are fighting so hard to have complete ownership over a woman's body. Do you have any idea what it is like to feel like you have no right to self-determination, to be told you're simply a vessel for a man's sperm? Because that is the reality women all across

America face, and it is a reality felt most strongly by women of color."

"You perform abortions here," I said.

Frank nudged her leg. She glanced down at him, and some of the stiffness eased from her shoulders. She resumed petting him and met my gaze unflinchingly. "That's not the only thing my clinic offers. But when that is what a woman comes to me wanting, yes. I do. I give her a far safer alternative to a fifth of whiskey, a hot bath, and a coat hanger."

"And what about Kimimela?"

She sighed and dropped her gaze, rubbing her forehead. "Annie approached me first. I had…helped her once before. She came to me, and I told her to bring her sister in. We'd do the tests to confirm the pregnancy, and then I would take care of it."

"Something changed," I guessed.

"I had never met Kimi before, only Annie, so I didn't know…" She swallowed. "Five years ago, a woman came to my clinic. A white woman from the west coast. Affluent, passionate about women's rights. I thought she might offer sponsorship. But instead…" Her voice faded.

"What did she offer?" I prompted when she remained quiet and her gaze remained on Frank.

"An alternative to abortions." Her gaze came back to mine. "I don't pressure any of the women who come to me looking for an abortion. If that's what they want, then that is what I provide. But for a few, I tell them about a different option available to them."

"What option is that?"

"Adoption," she said quietly. "But…not the kind

you're thinking of."

I thought of the files in the backpack. My initial thought had been the skin trade until I heard that Kimimela was pregnant. "I'm thinking of the black-market kind," I told her bluntly.

"Then you're right on track," she said. "For a few of my patients, I give them the option to go to Denver. That's the closest facility to us here, but they're all over the country. I vetted the place myself. It's not a back-alley operation. If the women and girls who come to me fit the profile, they're offered more money than most of them have ever dreamed of having."

"What makes them different from the others?"

"You have to understand, I don't do this for money. I don't get any kickbacks for sending them to Denver. I want what's best for these girls, because that's what they are. Most of the women who come to me for an abortion are babies themselves. These girls have used the money to go on to college. The baby trade has terrible connotations, but it's not all bad."

"What profile did Kimimela fit?" I asked.

She took a deep breath. "She could pass for white."

I thought about the files in Annie's backpack. How only a small percentage of the women were white. Most were Latina, black, or Native American. Given a golden ticket to a brighter future only if they looked white enough that their unborn child likely could pass for white as well.

"What happens if the baby isn't white enough once it's born?"

"I don't know," she admitted.

"And what happens if the women change their

minds about selling their babies?"

"I don't know that either," she said. "Did Kimi change her mind?"

"The autopsy report says she was pregnant, so I think she did." I leaned forward. "The emblem on your window matches the emblem on a stack of paperwork I have on at least fifty women. I need a name."

"I don't have one," she said. "I call a number after I've presented the option to my patient and they've agreed. Transport is arranged, and everything is handled on the other end."

"An organization like this would have a lot to lose if a woman changed her mind and decided to talk about what she'd been offered."

"Did they kill Kimi?" she asked softly.

"Someone strangled her to death in a cheap motel in a rough area of Denver. The cops have no leads. I'd say that's one way to silence someone who has decided she doesn't want the deal she was offered."

"Oh, Christ," she whispered, her hand covering her mouth.

"I need that number you call."

She nodded and stood, moving to her desk. She wrote the number on a piece of paper and offered it to me.

"I've only tried to help the women and girls who come to me." Sincerity and despair both weighed heavily in her voice. "I thought this could be a…a way out for them. You have no idea what poverty is until you've seen it on Pine Ridge."

"I believe you," I said. "But right now, that doesn't help Kimimela or Annie."

"Annie? What has happened to her?"

"She's missing," I said, and headed toward the door. I paused and looked back at the woman. "The facility outside of Denver was torched the night after Annie broke in and stole a number of their patient files. I'm not sure that number you've been calling will work any longer."

Jack was leaning against the shaded side of the red building when I passed back through Allen.

"A neighbor said a shiny black car showed up at the house one day and picked Kimi up," he said as he climbed into the passenger's seat. "No one saw her after that, and about a month after she left, a phone call came in at the service station. Charles, the man who owns the place, told me it was Kimi asking for Annie. She sounded real upset. The morning after Annie got the call, Charles's car was stolen. Annie hasn't been seen since."

I rubbed the back of my neck, mind racing. I thought about the black vehicle that had shown up in town, about the men who had chased Annie into the woods. "Did anyone take down a tag number on the vehicle that picked Kimi up?"

"No," Jack said. "They did notice that the driver was a woman, though. How did it go at the clinic in Kyle?"

"Annie's sister was pregnant. She arranged for Kimi to have an abortion, but the kid got a better offer."

Jack's eyebrows went up. "What kind of better offer?"

"Selling the infant."

For once, Jack had no response. His eyes went wide

and he looked away, rubbing his chin. Finally, he said, "The sheriff was right. We have no grasp on the kind of poverty the people deal with here."

"No," I agreed. "We're not going to find any more answers here. From what the woman at the clinic told me, Denver is only one small part of it. Annie could be anywhere."

"What do you want to do?" Jack asked.

I rubbed the back of my neck and stared out the window at the wasteland of Allen. "I think we need to go back home." I was missing something, something key, but I did not know what.

Thirty

JOAN

now

"I need you to show me where we left them," I said as soon as Donald walked in the front door.

"Jesus fucking Christ," he snapped. "Not this again."

I had asked a number of times throughout the year. I was not certain why I had needed to know where Winona and Emma were abandoned in the wilderness. Maybe to reassure myself of the distance between their decaying bodies and me. Although the miles between us had not protected me from being haunted by them.

Now I would not take his refusal for an answer.

"Show me where the mine is," I said.

For the first time in the last fifteen years, I did not flinch away from him when he thundered toward me. I held his gaze.

Strangely, it halted him in his tracks inches from me, his hand raised for a blow. Unlike the countless times before, he did not follow through. He stared at me, and his hand fell slowly to his side.

"Is this about the girl?"

This time I barely contained a flinch. The girl he did not realize was locked in our basement.

He hit me with a reminder of how much he had done for me as often as he struck me with his fist. But I knew now that fifteen years ago he had done what he did to protect himself. If he found out about Emma, he would kill me.

"Yes," I said. "I can't rest until I see…" I was not certain what I expected to see. There was no way a child as young as she was at the time could have freed herself from the restraints of the car seat and walked out of the mountains to safety. Someone must have found her, but I did not know why they had not reported finding a young child left in an abandoned shaft deep in the woods. "I need to see."

He must have been as disoriented by Emma's return to Raven's Gap as I was, because after a moment, he nodded. "Alright. We'll wait until dark."

This time, I did not close my eyes. I noted every turn. I filed away every landmark I thought I could recognize again in the daylight.

When he stopped the truck and we went the rest of the way on foot, I tried to memorize the route, even though there was no trail and the darkness felt as if it pressed against my skin and cut off my breath.

It took us a long time to find the mine shaft. The entrance was half collapsed now, and brush had grown up around what was left of the yawning mouth, hiding it from sight in the dark. Donald was only able to find it because he knew what he was looking for and where.

"I found this when I was hunting with my dad when

I was a boy," he said as we cleared away the brush.

I said nothing, putting all of my strength into yanking away the overgrowth.

There were no boards across what remained of the entrance. It looked like a hole in the ground, the long-forgotten den of some wild creature. Or the entrance to a tomb where two innocent people had been abandoned to rot.

I dropped to my hands and knees and crawled through, ignoring Donald's startled exclamation behind me.

I shoved the flashlight out in front of me, and it was everything that my nightmares had shown me. I had to crawl for about eight feet. My breath sawed in my lungs, and rubble rained down on me when my head brushed the earthen ceiling. I felt something drop onto the back of my neck and insectile feet scurry under my collar and down my back. I locked my teeth around a scream.

When there was finally enough room to stand, it took me two attempts to gain my feet I was shaking so hard.

Donald cursed behind me, and I could hear dirt showering him as he tried to navigate the cave's entrance. "Give me the light," he said.

I ignored him and moved slowly through the mine shaft. More collapses had occurred since we had been here that night. I had to climb over numerous piles of rubble along my trek. The support beams seemed to disintegrate before my eyes. This entire cavern would be lost to the mountainside soon. It was collapsing in small cascades of dirt and debris all around me.

I tucked my face into the bend of my elbow and smothered a cough. One loud sound, and I was afraid the roof would come down on my head.

I scrambled over a rock fall and froze when I reached the other side.

She was exactly where I had left her, still strapped into the baby carrier. Her clothes were rags now, the blanket I had knit merely a tatter. Her little hands and feet were gone. Her leg and arm bones were scattered around the mine's rough dirt floor. But her rib cage was still snuggly secured in the baby carrier.

I fell to my knees beside her. I was not certain if it was a scream, a sob, or vomit that crawled up my throat.

Donald stumbled to a halt beside me, breathing raggedly.

"There," he said. "Just as I thought. That kid claiming to be Emma is lying."

"It can't be," I whispered. I had been so certain. I had seen Winona's smile in hers, the strength of Hector's features in her face.

"We don't have anything to worry about," he said. "Now let's go."

"She's in our basement."

Silence met my words for several thundering heartbeats.

"What?"

"The girl. The one claiming to be Emma. She's in our basement."

"What do you mean?" Donald said slowly, and I could hear the anger building in his voice.

I tucked the tattered blanket I had knit so long ago

closer about what remained of Emma before I stood and turned to face him.

"The girl claiming to be Emma is locked in our basement."

He looked like a monster in the eerie gleam of the flashlight, all snarled mouth and hateful eyes. When he raised his hand, it seemed three times the size as normal, huge against the tight shadows that surrounded us.

The blow knocked me off my feet, and I fell backward in a sprawl over the baby carrier. It tumbled over, and Emma's small skull rolled away into the darkness.

"You stupid cunt," he breathed.

The punches and kicks came too swiftly to do anything but curl into a tight ball and close my eyes.

I deserve this. I deserve all of this. It had been my mantra for fifteen years. But when I felt a rib snap against the toe of his boot, my eyes flew open. The flashlight had rolled away. The light was cast against the earthen wall. And caught in the gleam of light, lying in the dirt, was Emma's small skull.

Anger snuffed out my mantra. I should have turned myself in fifteen years ago. I should have given that baby a chance at life and a future. I was not the only one responsible for this horror.

I tried to crawl away from the buffeting force of the blows.

He came after me, jerking me up to my knees with his hand clenched in the hair at the nape of my neck. I grappled for his wrist when I felt my scalp burn and tear.

"You ruin everything," he whispered.

I abandoned attempting to catch his wrist. With my fingers curled to claws, I struck out at him. I caught him hard across the face with a blow that was mainly made up of fingernails. His skin caught and tore under my nails, and he cried out in pain.

In the glow of the flashlight, his blood looked black as it spilled down his face.

He staggered backward. I slumped forward at the sudden relief in pressure on my scalp.

Donald stared at me. He slowly raised his hand and touched his ripped cheek. His eyes widened when he drew his hand away and saw his fingers stained with blood. He met my gaze, and I saw murder in his eyes.

When he took a lurching step toward me, I reacted, shoving him hard.

His arms wind-milled. The fury in his face morphed into fear as the earth dropped out from under him. He fell with a scream, and the echo sent a cascade of debris down on my head.

I ducked, hands clamped over my ears to block out the sound. But I still heard the wet, hollow thump of his body hitting the ground and his scream abruptly silenced.

Part III

Thirty-One

Hector

It was a long ten-hour drive back to Raven's Gap. Night had fallen, but the sky to the south glowed eerily.

I dropped Jack off at his truck.

"Thank you," I told him.

He paused. "We'll find her, Hector."

When I said nothing, he closed the door and got in his truck.

People kept saying that to me. *We'll find her*. They had said the same thing when my girls disappeared. The words were meaningless to me.

I executed a tight turn in the middle of the road and headed back across town to Maggie's. William's car was not in her driveway, but I parked and got out.

I did not even have a chance to knock. The front door opened as soon as I stepped on the porch.

Frank darted ahead of me. Maggie leaned down and rubbed his ears. When she straightened, he bounded into her house. I could hear Louie barking in greeting within.

"You look exhausted," she said.

I remembered the words I had hurled at her. *I'm not her father. It's not my fucking responsibility to protect her.*

"Come inside," Maggie said. "I made chili for dinner earlier. There's extra."

I followed her inside and took a seat at her kitchen table. She reheated a bowl of chili for me, and when she placed it in front of me, I looked up at her.

"You were right."

"No," she said. "I was wrong."

"I—"

Her hand caught mine in a tight grip. "I was *wrong*. You've been my closest friend for a long time now. You've always been there when I needed you. I should never have said that."

I stared down at our clasped hands. "I didn't know how to love Winona and Emma. I couldn't give them what they needed from me. What they deserved. I didn't…" My voice trailed off. "I didn't know how. I still don't."

She was silent for a long moment. "You care about me," she said finally.

I looked up and met her gaze. "You know I do."

She nodded. "You care about Frank."

The poodle lifted his head from my foot.

"I'd give my life for that dog," I admitted.

She smiled and her fingers tightened on mine. "It's not some intangible emotion. It's not some grand gesture. It's just a choice you make. To care about someone. To make them a priority in your life. I've seen you do that. You've done it for me."

"You make it sound so simple," I said.

Her voice was gentle. "It's not a transaction where you're left holding the bill. I think you know how to love just fine. If you didn't know how to do so all those years ago, you've learned in the last fifteen."

I ran my thumb over the back of her hand. "I think you have too much faith in me."

"Well, someone has to," she said.

I chuckled.

"Tell me what you found," she said. "William told me some of it."

She knew about the burnt home south of Denver and the young girl who had been found strangled to death in a seedy hotel in a rough area of town. I told her about the gut wrenching conditions Annie and her sister lived in, about the younger girl's pregnancy and the clinic on the reservation, about the option presented to the girls with just the right skin tone.

"A car almost hit her the day after she arrived," Maggie said suddenly. "I was coming out of the grocery store and heard squealing tires."

"I don't know why she picked me, but she must have thought I could protect her and help her give her sister justice."

"We've searched every day," Maggie said. "Evelyn made flyers and posted them here, in Gardiner, in Livingston, and even in Bozeman. I filed a missing person's report at the police station. William has been searching since he arrived. We *will* find her."

I turned my hand over in her grasp. "Hope is a dangerous, false thing," I said quietly. I remembered how certain I had been fifteen years ago that Winona and Emma would be found. How that certainty had been whittled away as the days and then weeks and months passed.

Her hand tightened on mine. “But it’s what we have right now, and I’m not letting go.”

She promised to update William and let him know I would meet him at the diner in the morning.

The inn was dark and locked up for the night when I returned. I let myself in the front door and moved through the great room toward the kitchen. Movement caught in the corner of my eye, and I turned to look out the back wall of windows. Frank whined, and when I looked over at him, I found him standing at the french doors leading outside.

I opened the doors and followed him onto the back deck. He went straight to the railing and let out a soft bark.

The white wolf lifted her head at the greeting. Her nose went up at the same time Frank’s did, both of them scenting the air.

The wind was shifting, blowing hard from the south, bringing with it the smell of Yellowstone smoldering. The smell was sharp in my nose, and it made my eyes water. Frank sneezed.

I stared at the red glow of the sky in the south. The change in the wind sent a prickle of unease over me.

I glanced back across the river, but the white wolf was gone.

Frank sneezed again.

“Inside,” I told him.

I locked the french doors behind us, but the smell followed me in. I needed to get my radio and check the updates on the fires in the park.

When I crossed the great room, I caught sight of the car parked on the street in front of the inn. It was a dark sedan.

"Stay here," I ordered Frank.

I exited the inn through the side door off of the dining room. I stopped long enough to grab a rock that edged the landscaping and then jogged up the drive.

I made no secret in my approach. The night was dark enough to conceal me, or whoever was in the vehicle was not paying attention. Either way, I walked right up to the driver's side and smashed the window with one blow of the rock.

"Jesus *fuck*!"

"Shit!"

The shouts were panicked from the two men inside the car. They both flinched, arms flying up to shield their faces.

I grabbed the driver by the collar, yanking him halfway out the window. I twisted so I could keep an eye on the passenger and pressed an edge of the rock against the back of the driver's head.

I looked past the pistol the passenger pointed at me. "Unless you want to wear your buddy's brains, I suggest you put that away."

"Do it, man," the driver said, voice shaking. "He's got a gun to my head."

The pistol wavered, and then the passenger tucked it away in a hidden holster.

"Turn the dome light on," I said, "and put your hands on the dash so I can see them." I nudged the rock against the back of the driver's head. "You put your hands on the roof."

With the dome light on, I could see it was the men from the woods. The driver's face was still grossly swollen and bruised from where I had kicked him. He had a bandage around his forearm from where Frank had torn into his flesh.

"Where is she?" They both remained silent, and I dug the edge of the rock harder into the back of the driver's head. "Where the fuck is she?"

"We don't know," the passenger said. "We've been looking for her for three days and haven't seen her anywhere."

"Why would we be here if we had her?" the driver asked, flinching away from what he thought was a gun pressed against his head. "Our orders weren't even to get the girl."

"Dave," the passenger warned.

The driver spoke over him. "All we were told to do was get the files she stole."

"From the facility in Cherry Hills Village," I said.

"Yeah," the driver said.

The passenger sighed and looked away. "Ah, hell."

"We lost her in Denver," the driver said, speaking quickly. "The girl was slick. She knew we were following her and just disappeared. We were still searching all over Denver when I caught sight of her on the news."

"You grabbed her in the woods," I reminded him.

"The girl pissed me off, okay?" he said. "All she told us was to get the files back. No one would believe the girl if she didn't have proof."

"Who is *she*?" I asked.

"Dave," the passenger gritted out. "Shut the fuck up."

His buddy listened to him this time. "I got nothing

else to say to you. We don't have the girl. If we did, we wouldn't still be here."

"Fair enough," I said.

I drew back the rock and cuffed him hard in the head. He went limp with a groan. I shoved the unconscious man back through the window into the driver's seat.

The passenger leaned back, moving his hands from the dash, but he did not reach for his gun. He met my gaze. "He deserved that," he said.

I dropped the rock. "Whoever she is, you tell her that if she wants the files from the facility in Cherry Hills, she can deal with me," I said.

He held my gaze for a long moment and then nodded. "You won't see us again."

I left him to deal with getting his unconscious partner out of the passenger's seat and headed back to the inn. Frank met me when I entered the front door and trotted at my heels as I headed into our apartment.

I went into the bedroom Annie had slept in and upended the room. The girl had only had her backpack, but I searched through the dresser. I lifted the mattress off the box spring, stripped the sheets, and looked under the bed.

I had boxed up much of what Faye Anders and her boy, Sam, had left behind and stored it in both closets. I searched the closets, but everything appeared to be exactly as I left it.

I fixed the bed and righted the dresser. I found nothing that told me anything about where the girl might have gone. She would not have run. I was convinced of it.

I need help, she had whispered tearfully in the lobby at the hospital.

Now she needed my help more than ever, and I was fucking failing her.

I strode into my bedroom. I had left the raggedy stuffed animal my daughter had carted everywhere leaning against my wife's skull. I fingered the stuffed rabbit's ear and then rested my hand on the curve of Winona's skull.

If Annie's disappearance was not linked to having uncovered the black-market adoption agency, I had no clue where to even start looking for her.

My thumb caught on the indention in Winona's skull at her temple. The only other thing that would put a target on the girl's back was announcing herself as my daughter.

I lifted Winona's skull and turned it over in my hands, studying the fractures in the bone at her temple and at the back of her head. The only person who would be threatened by the return of my daughter would be the person who murdered Winona.

The wail of a siren startled me awake in the early morning hours. Frank jolted upright, barking wildly.

I had not heard that sound in years. The haunting wail chilled me.

I dressed quickly and could already hear the inn's guests stirring. Evelyn met me in the kitchen.

"We have tornado sirens in the south," she said. "What's this siren for?"

"Fire," I said grimly. "Tell all the guests to stay calm

and start packing up. Vacation's over."

Everyone in town met in the parking lot of Thornton's Market. It was still dark. The only light on the horizon was the red orange glow to the south.

The twenty men from the volunteer fire department had brought one of their two firetrucks out, and the fire chief stood atop the engine.

"Where's Chief Marsden?" I heard someone ask. I glanced around and did not see the police chief anywhere.

"The wind has shifted," the fire chief shouted, "and the gusts are sending the fire straight toward us. It may shift again, but there's no guarantee. We've been given the order to evacuate."

"I'm not leaving!" came a call from the crowd, echoed by others.

The fire chief nodded. "My boys and I are ready to fight if it reaches town. We'll stay here 'til the tires start melting on the rigs."

"What can we do to prepare?" a woman asked.

"I'm urging everyone to leave," the fire chief shouted, ignoring the grumbles that met his statement. "But if you're not going to obey the evacuation order, get everything ready if the wind doesn't change and wet down your houses."

A hand tucked itself into my elbow, and I glanced down to find Maggie at my side. William stood beside her. His expression was grim when he met my gaze.

"Where's Frank?" she asked. Louie was clasped against her chest, his dark eyes wide and frightened. His little body trembled as the siren continued to scream its warming.

"At the inn. Evelyn is looking after him."

She nodded. Her own eyes looked wide and frightened. "It feels like '88 again."

"What can we do to help?" William called.

The fire chief nodded at him. "We've got a hundred firefighters coming into town today to help. We're going to be prepping a seventy-foot-wide fire line and starting a backfire. If you're staying and you've got an axe or a shovel, you can help."

"How bad do you think it's really going to be?" someone in the crowd asked. "We've been jerked around for a month by the Park Service waiting to hear."

The chief's face was weathered and lined. He looked grim and determined. There was little reassurance in his expression. "My advice is prepare for the worst. I always go into a fire expecting it to be hell."

Thirty-Two

ANNIE

It was dark when I woke up. I had no clue where I was or how I'd gotten here.

I lay on a hard, cold surface, and I could not even see the hand in front of my face.

"Hello?" I whispered. My voice disappeared into the dark.

I pushed myself up to my hands and knees. I felt unsteady and sick. I had to shove back the panic that crawled up my throat. I couldn't see a seam of light anywhere. There was no lessening in the absolute black that surrounded me.

"Hello?" I could hear the quiver in my voice. "Is someone there?"

My voice didn't echo, and I could sit upright. I strained my ears to hear and tentatively reached out a hand.

I turned a slow circle on my knees, hand outstretched, and felt nothing but emptiness around me.

It was as dark, still, and silent as a grave. I began to tremble.

I tried to remember where I had been, what I had been doing last, but my memories kept escaping my grasp. I remembered the grunt Ed had made as the bullet struck him in the dark. I remembered Betty's cut off cry from downstairs and the creak of footsteps coming up the stairs.

I struggled to recall if I had been grabbed from their home, but then the memory of wailing sirens and the cold light of a hospital waiting room and the weight of Hector's coat on my shoulders came to me. Everything else I could remember was fleeting. A gas station, a hand grabbing me, running.

I was still wearing my clothes. That didn't necessarily mean anything. I slipped my hand between my legs and pressed my fingers hard against my crotch. I wasn't sore and aching, tender from unwanted invasion, or sticky from semen and blood. It didn't feel like it had before, so I didn't think I had been raped.

But it didn't mean I wouldn't be. I had no clue where I was or who had brought me here.

I took stock of what I did know. My head ached. That was too soft a word, I decided. It felt like someone had parked their car on my head and the pain and pressure made it feel as if my skull was going to explode. I grimaced at the imagery and had to swallow against the vomit that threatened to crawl up my throat.

I crept a hand along my scalp until I encountered the tender lump just above my temple. It felt huge beneath my fingers, and I flinched at the gentlest touch. My hair felt stiff and matted around it, and my fingers came away tacky from drying blood. My stomach heaved, and the dizziness was even more unsettling in the dark. I felt like I was swaying back and forth, and even though I could not see the room spinning around me, it felt like the floor was tilting under me.

I had never been on a ship. I wondered if this rolling sensation was what it felt like at sea when the storms turned the water black and white and the waves were so high it looked like they would crash over the boat. My mind drifted as I thought about ships and the movement of the ocean. I had never even seen the ocean. I wondered if it looked like the plains.

I couldn't focus my mind on a single thought, and nausea crept up on me so quickly I barely had time to lean to the side before I threw up in my lap. Throwing up was violent and painful, and I held my head in my hands as I heaved to keep it from falling right off my neck.

I didn't realize I was crying until I felt the dampness as I used my sleeve to wipe my face. I crawled away from the mess I'd made. I didn't feel myself falling until my shoulder hit the hard, cold floor.

I hadn't fallen far, just from my hands and knees, crumbling to the side. It felt like it jarred my head as hard as if I had fallen from a three-story building, though, and I cried out as the pain stabbed through my temples. A flash of white cut across my vision. For a moment, I thought someone had turned a light on, but when I blinked, I realized I still could not see anything at all in the darkness.

I wondered suddenly if I was blind. I poked myself in the eye to confirm my eyes were open. A sob caught in my throat, but my head hurt too much to cry.

I needed to get up and figure out where I was. I needed to come up with a plan to get out of here. I needed to...

My mind drifted away from me again. I just needed to rest for a moment. I closed my eyes, even though it made no difference in the darkness. I would rest for a few minutes. I would let the churning in my stomach settle and the hammering in my head ease. Then I would figure this out.

I shivered against the cold floor. I wished I still had Hector's jacket.

I lay on the palette on the floor wearing every article of clothing I owned, wrapped in every blanket we had. Snow drifted through the hole in the roof, and the wind cut straight through the tarp I had used to patch the wall.

My teeth chattered so hard it felt as if my eyeballs were bouncing in their sockets. My breath frosted the air in front of my face.

Kimi hadn't come home in a month. I had searched everywhere for her, knocked on every door, flagged down every car that passed.

"Be careful, Annie," several people said to me under their breath.

They knew as well as I did who she was with.

I couldn't be careful. She was my sister. She was my responsibility, and I had made a promise.

A sound outside brought my head up. The soft slide of snow underfoot. The creak of the rotting steps.

I stared at the doorknob and clutched my grandmother's shotgun. I pushed off the blankets slowly. The surge of adrenaline in my system blocked out the cold. The shotgun was loaded. I always kept it loaded and close by now.

I crouched in the corner and brought the barrel up as the doorknob turned. My finger rested on the trigger.

The catch of breath, the sound of a sob being swallowed, reached me as the door opened a crack.

"Annie?" a quivering voice called, barely above a whisper.

I jerked my finger away from the trigger and set the shotgun aside.

My sister stood in the doorway.

"Kimi," I breathed. I crossed the space between us in two steps and pulled her into my arms.

She sagged against me, and the tears poured out of her.

"I'm sorry," she cried. "I'm so sorry."

"It doesn't matter," I whispered, stroking her hair. It was icy and stiff from the cold. "It doesn't matter. You're home now."

She didn't have a coat on, and she wasn't shivering.

I drew her inside and closed the door. She was like a doll, letting me move her to the pallet on the floor without putting up any protest. I hurriedly turned on the battery-operated lantern.

The light was harsh, and it highlighted the dark shadows under my sister's eyes. She looked like she hadn't eaten or slept in the month she had been gone.

Her feet were bare.

I had her curl up in the spot on the palette I had just vacated. I stripped off half of my own layered clothes and bundled her into them, piling the blankets over her.

Her feet were an angry red and swollen. I tucked one into my armpit, while I gently rubbed the other.

I knew it had to hurt, but she was silent, staring up at me with tears leaking from the corner of her eyes.

"I'm so sorry, Annie," she whispered.

"It doesn't matter, Kimi," I assured her, struggling to warm her feet. "All that matters is you're home. Everything's going to be fine."

She shook her head. "It's not." Her chin trembled. "I'm pregnant."

She sounded young and scared. Just like the little girl she was.

"I'm here for you no matter what," I said. "I'll help you with whatever you want to do."

She cried. I stripped off my own socks and boots and carefully slipped them over her feet before I lay down at her side. She burrowed into me, and I wrapped my arms as tightly around her as I could.

When I woke, I drifted. I could not manage to put enough strength into my arms and legs to push myself upright. The best I could do was roll to the side and vomit when the urge suddenly hit me.

I couldn't tell how much time had passed. Minutes or hours, days or weeks. I hurt. My head screamed in protest at any movement and any thought. The hurt was a hot pulse that took over my heartbeat and my breathing. Nothing else existed except for that heated thrumming.

No one came to check on me. Not that I knew of. Every time I opened my eyes, I touched my eyelid to assure myself my eyes were open. The darkness never changed.

But others came and joined me in the dark, visiting me when I was not strong enough to keep them away or strong enough to hold them to me.

My sister slipped away from me, disappearing into the mist. Sometimes she laughed when I called after her. Other times she cried. The young men slipped from the shadows and grabbed me again, their hard hands over my mouth and at my wrists and ankles.

Then my mother was there, and her palm was cool against my flushed cheek. She sang to me, the lullaby one I had struggled to remember the words for when I tried to sing it for Kimi. Her lullaby became my grandmother's chanting and the smell of burning sage. The smell of burning sage drifted until it was the choking stench of my grandmother's body rotting in the locked bedroom. She reached a hand out to me, and her skin fell away from her bones. *Why?* she wailed. *Why do you dishonor me and keep my spirit bound?*

I rolled over and vomited again, but I could only heave as my empty stomach spasmed and clenched painfully.

Hector visited me. He gazed down at me, face hard and cold. He shook his head. *You're not my daughter*, he said to me, voice a sneer. I reached out to him, but he turned away and left me in the dark.

"Hector," I whispered. "Hector."

"Emma," a voice said softly. It took me long moments to realize the voice was not in my pounding head.

My eyes flickered open, and I lurched away from

the hand reaching toward me. It seemed huge in the sudden light that I could see.

The movement drove a knife through my skull. I cried out in pain.

"Shh, Emma," the voice said. "Shh. You're okay."

The hand came toward me again, this time holding a cloth. My eyes slid shut as the cool, damp cloth bathed my face. My face was hot. It was burning with heat. I thought I might have a fever.

My vision swam sickeningly, threatening to tighten my stomach into revolt again. I squinted my eyes and peered past the hand.

Recognition stunned me. It was Joan. The woman from the police department. The woman who was so nice and so pretty in that white soccer mom kind of way.

Memories filtered back through my throbbing brain.

The woman who had stopped and picked me up on the side of the road when I was trying to get back to Betty and Ed's home and get my backpack. She said she needed to swing by her house first. All I could remember was walking through her front door. After that, there was nothing.

She realized I was staring at her, and she smiled. Her smile was kind, concerned, and one hand cupped my cheek while she gently wiped the hard, crusted blood from around my temple.

"How are you feeling, Emma? I didn't mean to hit you so hard."

I swallowed, struggling to make sense of her presence.

"Would you like some water?"

Her question made me realize how dry my mouth and throat were. I had to swallow several times before I could say yes.

She held my head up and held a water bottle to my lips. I tried not to gulp the water, knowing it might come back up, but the cold liquid felt so good in my mouth and throat. I drank too quickly and choked.

Coughing made black spots dance across my eyes, and I was winded and woozy when Joan eased me back to the floor and wiped the spilled water from my chin and throat.

"I wish you had never come back," she said softly. "I don't know how you made it out of that mine, but you shouldn't have come back."

Her words sent a chill through me, and my battered brain scrambled to make sense of them.

"I'm not Emma," I whispered.

She stroked my hair back from my face, her fingers catching in the snarls where my blood had dried and glued the strands together. I winced at the tug on my scalp.

"Everything is going to be fine. I just need to know how much you remember," she said.

She sounded so sane it frightened me.

"I'm not Emma," I whispered again.

She smiled. "We'll talk later. You need to rest."

I moved to push myself upright as she retreated, but the room spun around me. "I'm not Emma!" I called after her.

She closed the door, and I was swallowed by the darkness again.

—

"My name is Annie," I whispered. "I'm not Emma."

By now, it was a prayer. I had lost track of how many times I had opened my eyes and found Joan studying me. Maybe it had only been twice. Maybe it had been dozens of times.

"You shouldn't have come back, Emma," she said. "How did you escape? Just tell me what you remember."

If she hurt me trying to get me to answer, I didn't feel it. All I could feel was the hammer driving a spike deeper and deeper into my head. She brought water and light with her, though. The water I gulped down, even though I knew it would come back up. The light I wanted more and more as my vision darkened.

"Please," I whispered. "I'm not Emma. My head. Something's wrong with my head."

I thought I whispered that. I couldn't be sure any longer.

Her hands on my face were always as gentle as a mother's. "Rest," she said softly. "We'll talk later."

I couldn't lift my head. In the absolute darkness, I wondered if I had already died. My breath wheezed in and out of my lungs. I shivered uncontrollably, but I felt like a fire was burning just under my skin.

If I hadn't already died, I was going to. I was going to die here. No one would ever find me.

Hector would probably be glad to be rid of me.

I wasn't his daughter. He wouldn't spend night and day searching for me. That was for the real Emma.

Joan thought I was the real Emma, but I wasn't. I

was no one's Emma. My name was Annie. Annie Between Lodges. Without a home and without a family.

I didn't even have the strength to cry about it.

I drifted.

Thirty-Three

HECTOR

The backfires failed. The wind had the force of a whip, and the embers jumped the line. My face was black from soot, my voice raw from shouting.

Flames towered over Raven's Gap, bearing down on the town. Over the last three days, anger and stubbornness had given way to fear. I stood at an intersection in town and directed traffic as those who had not evacuated raced to flee town now.

The blare of horns brought my head around to see that the long line of cars heading out of Raven's Gap had come to a grinding halt when one car parked in the middle of the street.

I started toward the car. Joan shoved out of the driver's seat.

I had not seen her since returning to town, but Donald Marsden was still missing. According to Joan, the police chief had not come home from a meeting about the situation in Yellowstone days ago. In the chaos of the wildfire bearing down on Raven's Gap, any search efforts and investigation had been postponed.

Joan ran toward me. I swore when I caught sight of her face. She stumbled as she approached me.

I caught her elbow. "Are you alright?"

Her gaze searched mine, and she ignored the shouts and horns. Her husband had always been careful to leave marks where no one could see. Her face was raw and sickeningly bruised. I wondered suddenly at the timing of her husband going missing and the livid bruises painting her face.

The only time I had seen her look anything but perfectly put together was when she was under me. But now her clothes were stained and wrinkled, her hair was tangled and limp, and it looked like she had not slept in days.

"Here," she whispered, thrusting a bundle of fabric into my hands.

"What—"

"I'm sorry," she said. She caught the back of my neck and drew me down until she could press her lips against mine. She let me go so quickly I stumbled in surprise. "I'm so sorry. I thought she was Emma. There might still be time."

She turned and ran back to her car. I heard the gears grind as she slammed it into drive, and then the long line to evacuate the town began to move again.

I looked down at the bundle she had shoved into my hands. It took me a moment to recognize what I held, it was so out of place. She had given me my own coat. A coat I had not seen in days. The coat I had wrapped around Annie's shoulders in the hospital the night she had disappeared.

Confusion left me reeling. How did she have my

coat? What was she apologizing for? The bruising on her face flashed through my mind, the fact that the chief of police was missing.

Those words she had spoken came back to me.

I thought she was Emma.

At some point between escaping the vehicle of the man who had picked her up at the gas station and reaching Raven's Gap, could Annie have gotten into Joan's car? If she had, why had Joan not brought her to the hospital or to the inn?

I thought she was Emma.

I could not process the implication of those words. It made no sense. And then I recalled the thought that had struck me: The only person who would be threatened by the return of Emma would be the person who murdered Winona.

Realization struck me so hard I stumbled.

"Fuck," I breathed. If my daughter's return was a threat to her, it meant Joan knew exactly what had happened to Winona and Emma. How was it even possible? As far as I knew, Joan and Winona had never been friends. I thought of the police chief and his disappearance. Was Donald responsible? Had I been working for the very man who had stolen my girls from me?

I was shaking, I realized, standing blindly in the middle of the road with horns and shouts blaring around me. An explosion split the air, echoed with screams around me, and I ducked, shaken out of my stupor.

I stumbled, catching my balance on the hood of a car crawling passed me.

There might still be time.

Did that mean Annie was still alive? I did not know, and I only knew of one place to look. If she was alive, if she was there, Annie was directly in the fire's path.

I left my post directing traffic and ran, ignoring the hammering on horns as I darted between the cars packing the two-lane road, all of them fleeing town. When I reached Maggie's house, she was tossing a suitcase into the trunk of her car. William was helping hold the line with the firefighters to give residents time to escape.

Louie and Frank were sitting in the front seat of her car.

"What—?" Maggie straightened as I ran up her drive.

"Keys," I gasped, winded from breathing smoke as I ran. My chest worked like a bellows, and my heart raced even faster than my feet had. "Annie. I think I know where Annie might be."

Her eyes widened. She scrabbled in her pocket and tossed me the keys to my truck. I snatched them out of the air.

I moved to the passenger's side of Maggie's car. Frank stuck his head through the cracked window. I leaned down and pressed my forehead to his. He whined.

I stroked a hand over his ears and straightened. Maggie moved to my side, her face tight with fear and concern.

"Don't let him come after me," I said. "Get in the car and get out of here."

She caught my elbow. "Hector," she whispered. "No."

"I have to. If there's any chance, I have to go back for

her."

"Where is she? I can go with—" A propane tank somewhere on the opposite side of town exploded with a resonate *boom*. Maggie flinched.

"Take Frank and get out of here while you still can. I'll be right behind you."

Her gaze searched my face and then she leaned into me, wrapping me in a hug so tight my chest felt constricted. Frank whined in the front seat of her car. "I can't believe I'm saying this, but please don't be a fucking hero."

I hugged her back just as tightly and laughed into her wiry, closely trimmed hair. "When have I ever been a hero?" I asked.

"I didn't think it was something I ever had to worry about," she admitted. Her voice was clogged with tears.

She flinched in my arms at the sound of another explosion.

I set her back from me. "Go," I said.

I waited until she was in her car and the engine roared to life. I turned and sprinted for my truck in the whirlwind of cinders and ash. The engine roared as I spun a quick U-turn. Both lanes of the state road were filled with traffic evacuating out of town. I plowed down the shoulder, truck rocking on the uneven ground.

The sky was black through a red haze as I raced back into Raven's Gap. My headlights did little to cut through the darkness. I almost missed the lane to the Marsden house and cranked the wheel hard, making the turn with a squeal of tires.

I could not see the flames when I slammed the truck

into park at the front steps of the house. The woods around the house stood tense and still, gallant and fearless.

Fear threatened to choke me, though, as I grabbed a flashlight, bounded up the deck, and kicked in the front door.

"Annie!" I shouted. "*Annie!*"

The house was silent. I searched every room, every closet, calling for her. The place was empty.

I almost missed the door leading down to the basement.

I jerked it open. The power was out, so the switch at the top of the stairs was useless. I clicked on the flashlight and followed the beam of light down the stairs.

I played the light over the large space. It was unfinished, cinderblock walls and concrete floors. It looked like it was used as a laundry room and a workroom. Tools and a table in one corner of the large space, a washer and dryer in the other.

In the furthest back corner of the room was a padlocked door. I did not know what it might have once been used for, but I had a sinking feeling I knew what it currently held.

I grabbed a long, heavy wrench from the workbench and approached the door. It took me two swings to break the padlock. I tossed the wrench aside and yanked open the door.

My light played over a hand-hewn rocking horse and cradle, a changing table and a rocking chair. And the girl curled on her side on the floor.

"I'm here, I'm here." It was almost a sound that was less than a whisper, but Annie repeated it over and over again. She had heard me yelling for her, I realized.

I fell to my knees at her side. The room was small and dark, and it smelled of piss, vomit, shit, and fear.

I tamped a tight lid on my rage. She still repeated, "I'm here, I'm here."

I placed a hand on her shoulder, and she went completely still, like a small wild creature freezing in the sights of a predator. "I'm here, Annie. It's Hector." I brushed her hair carefully back from where it had fallen to cover her face.

"Hector?" The word was soundless, but I saw my name on her cracked lips when they moved.

"I have you," I said. "I'm getting you out of here."

Her clothes were soiled but intact. The only injury I could see was a livid knot on her head.

How long she had been without food or water, I did not know. She cried softly as I lifted her into my arms, cradling her against my chest. I could not stop to comfort her. I could smell the smoke seeping into the house. Her head lolled against my shoulder, and she felt painfully light.

"It's alright now," I whispered. "I have you."

I took the stairs three at a time. Smoke was already filling the house. The roar of the flames in the distance raised the hair on the back of my neck. Suddenly I was back in my Airstream watching the flames eat across the ceiling over Frank and me as we crouched on the floor amidst a flurry of bullets.

I shook myself and ran from the house.

Outside was hell. The trees in the distance were ablaze, and the line of fire marched steadily toward us, eating through everything in its path.

I ran to my truck. I shoved the seat back so I could keep her in my arms and threw the ignition into reverse. I turned tightly, the truck rocking to a halt before I shifted into drive and stomped on the gas. The truck roared down the drive back toward town, but when I rounded the bend, I slammed on the brakes. The wind had spread the fire too quickly. A wall of blaze blocked my route into town. The inferno was all around us.

The tree fell as if in slow motion, branches ablaze. I clutched Annie tightly to me, burying my face in her hair as I braced for the impact.

The windshield exploded as the tree landed on the hood of my truck, and we were jolted so hard that my head hit the roof. Annie cried out in fear.

When the truck stopped shuddering and rocking, I kicked open the door and staggered to the ground. The heat of the fire felt as if it were searing the flesh off my bones.

Annie whimpered in my arms. I clutched her close. "I've got you," I assured her.

I ran, cutting through the woods, lungs burning. The fire howled at my back, and I ran as quickly as I could without risking falling. It was like night in the smoke.

Movement at my side startled me, and my heart sank. I thought at first it was Frank, but when the canine raced ahead of me, I realized it was not my poodle. It was the white wolf, her hair singed and stained with soot.

I veered through the woods, aiming back toward town, but I staggered to a halt when the wolf cut so close in front of me, I almost tripped over her. I took another step. Again, she cut off my path.

She stood in front of me, teeth bared in a soundless snarl.

I stared at her, searching for the color of my wife's deep brown eyes in hers. But the wolf's were golden yellow.

She stared back at me, and when she turned and ran, this time I followed her. She led me away from town, deep into the woods.

In the dark, with the smoke staggering my lungs and the flames howling at my back, I was lost. My eyes burned and wept. I kept a hand on the back of Annie's head, pressing her face against my shoulder to try to spare her the worst of it.

I did not realize the wolf was leading me to the river until I stumbled into the water.

The river ran cold but wide and shallow here. The wolf appeared before me through the dense, heavy fog of smoke. She stared at me, gaze keen and sharp.

"Go," I whispered, voice hoarse. The roar of the fire approached at my back. "We're safe now." I was not certain if that was entirely the truth.

She turned, darted up the far riverbank, and was gone.

This time, I did not follow her. I forded upriver, stumbling over the smooth waterworn stones. The inferno blazed a path through the forest. Around the next bend, the river narrowed and deepened.

"You came for me," Annie murmured. Her voice was a mere croak.

I clutched her tightly to me as I staggered when a rock rolled underfoot. "Don't try to talk."

She shook in my arms.

I almost went under when I rounded the bend and

the riverbed fell suddenly away from me. I could see the inn in the distance on the riverbank, and beyond it, Raven's Gap burning.

The trees along the riverbank beside us went up in flames.

"Hold your breath," I whispered to Annie.

She nodded against my chest. I sucked in a raw, smoky breath and sank below the water.

Thirty-Four

ANNIE

The motel room door was cracked. When I put my hand on it and it creaked open, dizziness hit me. I put a hand on the doorframe to steady myself. My breath hurt my throat and rushed in my ears.

The room was dark, but I stepped inside resolutely.

"Kimi? I'm here. Where are you?" My voice shook.

There was no response.

I felt for the light switch along the wall but could not find it. I shuffled carefully to the bedside table and twisted the toggle on the lamp.

I wished I hadn't as soon as the light pierced the room. The motel was in the worst part of Denver, a pay by the hour kind of place where people looked the other way. It looked like a lot had happened in this room in the hours it had been rented in the past, if the stains on the floor and the holes in the wall were anything to go on. From the corner of my eye, I saw something scurry along the wall.

I shuddered. "Kimi?"

I rounded the bed slowly, eyes on the dark yawn of the

bathroom door.

I tripped over her legs.

I went down hard, head bouncing off the dresser. The crack of pain barely registered as I caught sight of Kimi.

"No, no, no, no, no." I wasn't sure if I whispered or screamed as I crawled across the dirty floor.

She looked like she was sleeping, face slack and serene. Her eyelashes were a dark fan in her colorless face, and she appeared small and fragile. The dark bruises around her throat were shaped like fingers.

I knew without touching her she was gone. The first sob felt like it ripped my throat as I gathered her gently against me. Her head fell forward, heavy and limp against my shoulder. I held her tightly and pressed my face into her hair to keep the screams that were clawing their way up from my chest from getting loose.

I heard my name called. I stirred, wondering if the spirits had come for me.

"I'm here," I whispered. "I'm here."

I thought I would be afraid at the end, but all I felt was relief. My skull was splitting open like an overripe piece of fruit. The pain was so fierce that when I gathered enough strength to lift my hand and touch my head, I was surprised that my fingers didn't sink straight into my brain. It felt like every protective layer had been stripped away and my head was reduced to pulsing, throbbing gray matter.

Suddenly, there was light, and I flinched away. I'd heard there was light at the end, but I wished it weren't so bright.

"I'm here," I whispered to the spirit behind the light.

Don't leave me here, I wanted to beg. *Take me away*

from this place.

But all I could manage was another, "I'm here."

A hand landed on my shoulder, and I went still. *I'm ready*, I told myself. But a small part of me shrank away from the finality of it.

"I'm here, Annie. It's Hector."

My hair was brushed back from my face.

Hector. Hector wasn't a spirit. My lips moved over the shape of his name. *Hector*. He wouldn't be here. I wasn't Emma. I was just Annie. I wasn't his daughter. Just someone who was lying to him.

"I have you," he said. "I'm getting you out of here."

It made no sense. Hector wouldn't be here. Not for me. I had no one to search for me, no one to rescue me. I was going to die here in the darkness alone.

But it wasn't so dark now. There was a light. And I wasn't alone. Hector was here.

I cried out as he lifted me into his arms. His arms felt real around me. Real and strong and solid. My head was too heavy to hold up. I rested it against his shoulder. That felt real, too.

"It's alright now," Hector said. "I have you."

There was smoke and heat. A jolt that felt like it would send my head rolling right off my neck.

Hector's arms were tight around me. He ran, and every step jolted me, driving that spike in my brain deeper and deeper.

He had come for me, and hell was all around us.

I tried to cling to him, but there was no strength in my arms and hands.

He had come for me.

"Don't try to talk," Hector said.

Moments later, he told me to hold my breath.

Then there was nothing but cold, wet silence.

"Help me!" a voice shouted. "I need help here!"

Hector. He needed help. I had to help him. He had come for me.

I tried to open my eyes, but they were too heavy. I tried to lift my head, but it was caught in a vice. Hector needed my help. I couldn't let him down. He had come for me.

More shouts swirled around me, and then the air was battered by noise and wind.

I was jolted. I cried out.

"Be careful with her!" Hector snapped, voice hard and sharp.

Hector. He needed help. I had to help him.

"I'm coming in the chopper with you," he said.

Someone protested, but the wind suddenly lessened, even though the noise was relentless. It whipped through my fractured head like a tornado I had watched cross the plains once. Devastating, shredding everything in its path.

A hand grasped mine. Large, rough fingers caught mine and held on.

"I'm here, Annie," Hector said.

"She probably can't hear you, sir," someone said.

I wanted to tell them they were wrong. I could hear him. He had come for me. I had heard him calling.

"I'm here, Annie," he said again. "You're going to be okay. I'm here."

I would have clung to his fingers if I could. My hand

wouldn't work, though, so I clung to his words.

I couldn't breathe.

I gagged and fought against the obstruction in my throat.

"Just relax, honey," an unfamiliar voice said. "You're intubated. We're going to do your breathing for you."

They weren't doing it good enough. I couldn't breathe. They were sawing my head off. I could feel it. The grating whine of pain. The sharp teeth of a blade against my skull.

I struggled, reaching for the tube I could feel between my lips. I needed to tell them I couldn't breathe and my head was about to explode.

"Sir, you can't—"

"Annie."

I went still at the sound of his voice. It was raw and hoarse and almost soundless, but I heard it, and I clung to it. He was here. He had come for me.

I couldn't get my eyes open. The lights were too bright overhead. My eyes were too swollen, and I could feel dampness streaming over my temples.

"I'm here, Annie," he said again.

I felt the weight of his hand rest on my forehead. It should have been too much, with the pressure expanding and tightening in my head. But instead, it felt like the weight of his hand was the only thing keeping my skull intact. *Don't let go*, I wanted to tell him. *Don't leave me.*

"I'm right here. I'm not going anywhere."

The fight went out of me. I sagged, and the chaotic

beeping that pierced my skull slowed. The shouting receded to a murmur.

"Sir, you really can't be back here," a voice said.

"Try to remove me," Hector said.

I let go, drifting on the current of voices around me, anchored by the hand resting on my forehead.

Thirty-Five

HECTOR

I paced the hospital hallway outside the intensive care unit.

Annie had begun seizing on the helicopter ride to Bozeman. She had another seizure as soon as we arrived at the hospital.

Despite my protests, she had been rushed away from me, and I was left standing there staring after her small form on the gurney. I shrugged off the nurse trying to guide me to the emergency room to be checked over and paced until the pediatric neurosurgeon that had been called in sought me out.

"Her brain is swelling with nowhere to go," she told me, voice blunt but gentle. "We've infused her with pentobarbital. Basically, we've put her brain to sleep to help lower the amount of blood flow it needs. But the intracranial pressure keeps climbing. If it continues to do so, she's at risk for a brain herniation."

"What will that do?" I demanded.

"It could lead to a stroke or to damage to her brain stem."

"It could kill her," I said, and I moved to a chair to sit down before my knees gave out.

"Very easily," the neurosurgeon confirmed. "I want to do a decompressive craniectomy. I'm going to remove part of her skull so she will continue to have blood flow and oxygen to her brain and to help minimize the pressure and swelling."

I flinched. "You're going to cut her head open?"

"I'm going to remove a bone flap on the left side of her skull to begin with," she said. "I may need to put a drain in the ventricles of her brain, but I won't know until I get in there."

"I want you to do whatever it takes to save her," I said.

She placed a hand on my shoulder. "I intend to. My team is one of the best in the country."

It had taken hours of surgery and then several more hours had passed before I had been allowed to see her.

"Her ventricles are small, and I was concerned about increased swelling," the neurosurgeon said as she stood by my side. "I took bone from the front and back of her skull as well."

She looked so small and wounded in the bed with her head elevated, tubes protruding from her, a machine breathing for her, and her skull swaddled in bandages.

"Is she going to be okay?" I asked.

"We're monitoring her ICP levels, her intracranial pressure. We'll have a better sense of things over the next few hours."

I took a hesitant step toward the bed and carefully touched Annie's fingers.

"She's a strong kid," the neurosurgeon said softly.

I nodded and waited until her footsteps retreated.

"I'm here, Annie," I whispered. "You're not alone."

The nurses were strict about visiting hours in the ICU, and Annie was heavily sedated. When I was asked to leave for the night, I resumed my pacing in the hall.

The sharp, steady rap of heels against the polished floors reached me. I glanced at the clock on the wall. The hands showed it was just after three in the morning.

The woman who came around the corner was polished, and her clothes looked like they had cost more than my Airstream. Everything about her shouted *wealth*. She was out of place in a hospital in Montana.

I thought I knew exactly who she was.

She confirmed it when she approached the nurse at the desk outside of the unit. "I'd like to see Annie Between Lodges, please." Her voice was as rich as her appearance.

"No."

Both the woman and the nurse turned to me.

"No," I repeated. "I don't want this woman allowed anywhere near her."

The nurse had just come on shift in the last thirty minutes. She rustled through the charts on her desk. "And you are—"

"Her father," I lied.

The woman's arched brow and slow smile said she knew I lied, but instead of arguing, she turned back to the nurse. "Thank you, I'll just speak with Annie's father."

She walked past me, and I followed her down the hall until we were well away from the waiting area and nurse's desk.

She did not offer an introduction. "You have me at a disadvantage. Although perhaps I should have claimed I was her mother."

"What do you want?" I asked bluntly.

"I'm not here to hurt her," she said, "but she has something of mine I would like returned to me."

"She doesn't have the files any longer," I said.

Her gaze sharpened on me. "I see. Is there some place more private we can talk?"

"The cafeteria should be open." It would be empty at this hour.

"Very well." Each click of her heels on the tile was crisp and precise as I followed her to the bank of elevators.

I studied her as the elevator descended. Not a hair was out of place, not a wrinkle marred her skirt suit. She reminded me a bit of Joan.

My mind shied away from the thought. I could not think about Joan right now without wanting to tear something apart with my bare hands. She had come to me, all those years ago. She had come to the very bed I had shared with Winona, and she had known exactly why Winona was no longer in it. She had to have.

I'm so sorry. I thought she was Emma.

I shook my head and focused again on the woman before me.

She studied me with equal appraisal. When the elevator doors opened, I gestured for her to go ahead. She smiled.

"Are you an old-fashioned man, Hector?"

I had never told her my name. "Not particularly. I'm not polite, either. You just don't seem to be a woman someone should turn his back on."

Her smile was warm and charming, and it caught me off guard. "I can tell I'm going to enjoy this conversation. Which way to the cafeteria?"

I pointed and followed slightly behind her. She surprised me by showing no hesitation at filling a paper cup with coffee that smelled like burnt oil. She picked a table in the far corner of the room, and I watched as she dumped five individual creamers in her coffee before stirring it and taking a sip.

"I've had worse," she said.

I took a drink of mine black and grimaced. "I hope you've had better, too."

"You do know she's not your daughter?"

It seemed she knew more than just my name. "I know who she is, and I know who you are."

She tilted her head. "And who am I?"

"You have a pen?"

She reached into her purse and slid a thin, gold pen across the table to me. I drew a rough representation of the emblem that watermarked the files and again on the clinic in Kyle.

I placed the pen and napkin in front of her, and she covered the emblem with a manicured hand.

"Will fifty thousand do?" she asked.

"I don't want your money," I said. "I want information."

"Ah, something more valuable than cash."

"You wanted to talk," I reminded her.

She took a sip of her coffee and did not even flinch. "That I did." She tapped a polished finger on the napkin. "Do you know what this logo represents?"

"A baby selling operation."

"Choice. It represents choice. That is what I offer women."

"Only if their skin is not too brown," I pointed out.

She smiled again, and this time it held a sharper edge. "I am simply on one side of the equation, supplying what the consumer demands."

"That's a cold way of looking at it."

"Only if you have placed me in a position as a savior, and I'm not running a charity. I'm a businesswoman, nothing more."

"How many of these facilities do you have?"

"One less than what I did have," she said. "The situation with Kimi made things difficult for us at the Denver location."

"And do you usually have situations that become difficult?"

"Our nondisclosure clause in the contract is very, very clear, and we make certain the girls understand exactly what they are signing. We've had a few back out, which is understandable. The reason they accepted the offer is because they did not want to be mothers at that point in their life. When you carry a fetus to term, even if you are giving it away, you can never escape the fact that you are a mother. Your body and your mind bear those scars forever."

"They're not giving it away. They're selling it."

She lifted her coffee cup in a salute. "Touché. But you're a man, so I don't expect you to understand the burden of motherhood."

I nodded that point to her. "When they back out, what happens?"

"We provide them the abortion they initially wanted. They have to pay back the advance they received. We go over the nondisclosure clause again, and that is that."

"What if they ignore the nondisclosure clause?"

"They don't. They understand what's at stake. Not just for them, but for other women in their same position."

"But you thought Kimi would ignore it," I pointed out.

"Kimi was very young," she said carefully. "Sometimes that lack of maturity makes young girls do foolish things."

"So you had her silenced."

She chuckled, low and sweet. "I'm flattered by the assumption, but I'm not a mob boss running a crime ring."

"Just a businesswoman running a black-market adoption agency."

"That's a harsh term, but if you want to boil it down to that, it's not inaccurate." She leaned forward, resting her elbows on the table and folding her arms over one another. If anyone could personify ruthlessness and elegance in one package, she certainly achieved it. "Let me explain something to you. It's hard for men or even women who have not been in this situation to understand. My business is about choice, and that is something few women have. Society has always ground women under its heel. We are the baby makers of the patriarchy, and little more. There will always be those in positions of power who throw all of their effort into limiting the few rights women have been able to carve out for themselves. It doesn't matter what laws are put in place. Women will find a way, just like we've done for millennia. There will still be abortions. There will still be infants left in plastic bags in the woods. That's reality, Hector. A woman's reality. I'm simply providing an alternative to the back-alley butchers and leaving an infant in a public bathroom."

You ruined my life. I should have drowned you in the toilet after I had you. I sat back in my chair to absorb the blow of memory and my mother's words.

She must have seen something on my face, because her own softened. "I'm providing women safety, choice, and the money to determine their own course. Is that something you really want to stand against?"

"Not at all," I said. "But I do take exception to a twelve-year-old girl being murdered for that and her sister being threatened over it. So here is what I propose."

Her eyebrows rose and she sat back in the chair. "Go on."

"I'm keeping your files. You're a businesswoman. Call it insurance. I won't do anything with those files as long as you stay away from Annie. You walk away from her as if you had never heard of her before. She never hears from you again."

Her gaze searched my face. "That's your bargain."

"That's it," I agreed.

"And I just have to trust you?"

"I can't offer you more than my word," I said.

She smiled. "One of my favorite memories from my childhood is watching old westerns with my father. They were his favorite. You remind me of those shows I used to watch with him. All about honor and codes and dying by the sword."

"I believe they usually died from a gut shot."

She laughed. When her laughter tapered off, she studied me for a long, silent moment. "Alright. We have a deal. You keep your insurance policy, and as long as you never use it, you'll never see or hear from me again."

"As long as we never see or hear from you again, I won't need to use it."

She finished the last of her coffee and stood.

"There's one more thing," I said when she would have walked away. She turned back, one eyebrow arched. "I want a name."

She stared at me for a beat and then reclaimed her seat.

"I'm going to be accommodating with this demand, because you'd be doing us both a favor. I run a tight operation, but it's a clean one."

"I take it your man wasn't supposed to kill a little girl."

Her mouth tightened. "Let's just say he went off script without permission, and he knows it."

"He's in the wind, then."

She nodded. "All I can give you is a name."

"That's all I need."

The air was so thick in Louisiana I felt like I needed to chew it before I could take a breath.

I waited late into the night. The lights did not go out until well after midnight. I crept from my hiding place and approached the trailer.

When I had searched it earlier today, I found two pistols and a sawed-off shotgun. I emptied the magazines from the handguns and pocketed the shells from the shotgun. If he had another weapon, it was one he carried on him. It was a gamble I had to take.

He had no dog to sound the alarm, and he was so far from civilization, he did not bother locking his door. The air inside the trailer was stale and still. The interior was nearly barren. A threadbare couch that sagged in the middle against one wall, a mattress on the floor in the bedroom. I had walked the route from the front door to his bedroom several times today to ensure I did not need a flashlight.

He snored. I could hear the wet gurgle of noise before I reached his doorway. I didn't see the beer bottle left on the floor until I accidentally kicked it across the sticky tiles.

His snore choked off as he lurched upright, the gun he kept under his pillow in hand. Before I could react, his finger tightened on the trigger.

The gun clicked.

He squeezed the trigger three more times. *Click, click, click.*

I flicked the switch on the wall, and the bare bulb sputtered to life. No sense in standing here in the dark now that he knew I was here.

He stared at his gun as if it were a lover who had betrayed him. "What the—?"

"I removed the bullets when I was here earlier," I said helpfully.

"What do you want?" he asked warily.

He did not match his surroundings. Ray Culver was clean cut, neat, and trim. He looked like an actuary. He didn't sport the beer gut, stained wife beater shirt, or the lice-infested beard I had expected when I first found his trailer. But the trailer said he knew he had fucked up and was doing his best to lay low.

"To talk about Kimi Between Lodges," I said.

"Shit." He grimaced and tossed his gun aside. He scrubbed his hands over his face. "Look, things just got out of hand. I was having a rough day. My wife told me she's leaving me. For the guy who works at the local butcher shop. I was just going to talk to the girl."

I remained quiet, and he rushed to fill the silence.

"I'm not hired muscle. That's not how she runs things. I'm a lawyer. I just wanted to remind her of the nondisclosure. But she went ballistic, shrieking about how I was there to kill her. I snapped, okay? It happens. But I was careful and I made sure nothing would come back on the agency. That's why she sent you, isn't it?"

I ignored his question. "Do you know how old she was?"

His throat bobbed as he swallowed, and his eyes darted to his shotgun leaning against the wall in the corner. "I don't know. Look, man—"

"Twelve," I said. "She was twelve years old."

I wanted to tear him apart. I needed violence and a release from this pressure that had been growing inside me from the moment Joan had stumbled toward me and said those words.

I'm so sorry. I thought she was Emma.

I needed to know what had happened. What had Joan witnessed? What had Donald done to my girls? I had no answers, just as I had for the last fifteen years, but the rage was growing out of check now.

But beating this man to a pulp would only bring trouble. I offered him the pen and notepad I had purchased. The pen was still in its package from the store.

"Wh-what's this?" he asked, gaze locked on the gloves encasing my hands.

"This is your suicide, Ray. Now hurry up and write your note."

Thirty-Six

JOAN

Sometimes the weight of secrets was too heavy to bear. I felt hunched under the weight of the last fifteen years.

What have you done? Donald's words echoed in my head.

My steps dragged. The pistol I had taken from Donald's desk was cold and heavy in my hand.

I had intended to leave and forget everything about Raven's Gap. But then I had seen the children as the town was evacuated. The way they clung to their fathers' hands, the way they sought their mothers, the terror and confusion etched on their faces.

I thought about the child locked in the storeroom in my basement. Hector's coat had been around her shoulders when I picked her up along the side of the road. It was neatly folded in the passenger's seat of my car as I evacuated. When I passed him directing traffic, I remembered the way Winona's arms had convulsed around Emma when I struck her.

I had put my car in park before I even realized I had made a decision.

The only thing I had wanted out of life was children of my own. I had killed one already. I found myself unable to abandon another one to death.

I wondered if Hector had reached her in time. I wondered if I had been too late and they both perished in the fire. Just in case, I had left something for him on the seat of my car where I had parked it.

I found the mine's entrance quicker this time. I clicked on my flashlight and crawled into the tomb. It looked like animals had been inside recently, probably drawn to the smell of Donald.

I did not approach the vertical shaft to see if my light could penetrate all the way to the bottom.

I knelt by the car seat and gently lifted what remained of Emma free from the straps. I swaddled her in the blanket I had knit all those years ago. Her little skull rested against a pile of rocks. I tucked it into the crook of my elbow, tugging the blanket up around the curve of bone.

"There now," I said softly, cradling her in my arms.

I leaned back against the wall hewn out of the earth. A shower of dirt fell on my head, but I did not brush the debris aside. It reminded me of how people tossed dirt on a casket at a burial.

I placed the flashlight on the ground beside us and rested the pistol on my knee.

The last time I had sung the lullaby was here fifteen years ago, when the skeleton in my arms had been an innocent little girl I left alone in the dark to die. I had not allowed myself to even hum it since then, but now I sang softly.

In my mind, I could hear Emma whimper. I rocked her, patting her soothingly, and waited for my light to fade.

Epilogue

October 13th

HECTOR

I climbed down from the roof when I heard the truck approaching. Frank sat up from where he was sprawled on the front porch.

"Stay," I told him when I recognized the vehicle.

Grover Westland, the county coroner, lifted his hand in greeting as he approached.

"Now this is something," he said as I approached.

I turned and studied the view he was admiring.

The cabin was not on the ridge but instead built on the burnt stretch of meadow where my Airstream had once stood. It was much smaller than the one Winona had dreamed of. Two bedrooms instead of four, two bathrooms instead of three. The kitchen was a simple affair, but the wraparound porch was exactly what she had wanted.

She had been right: a kid needed a house to grow up in.

"I heard you were offered a job again," he said.

"Doesn't suit me any longer," I said. The police department held no appeal to me. Instead, when the search and rescue organization had approached me last month, I had accepted a position as an SAR trainer.

"Can't say I blame you there. I'm looking forward to retirement myself," Grover said. He turned from admiring my plot and met my gaze. "They found Joan. Self-inflicted gunshot wound to the head." I knew there was more when he reached out and clasped my shoulder bracingly. "They found her in an abandoned mine shaft that wasn't on any map. When they found her, they also found the rest of Winona's remains and Emma's as well. Donald's body was found, too."

I looked away, blinking against the sudden burning of my eyes. It was a long moment before I could speak. "I'll get you her skull." I swallowed. "I'd like them cremated, together."

"I'll make sure it's done," he said. He hesitated and then drew an envelope from his pocket. "You'll understand we had to open it, but this is for you."

"Thank you for coming out to tell me."

He gripped my shoulder for a long moment before releasing me. "I've had my doubts about you over the years, Hector, but this was never one of them."

As his truck disappeared around the bend, I climbed onto the porch and sat beside Frank. The poodle shifted until his chin rested on my knee.

I unfolded the paper in the envelope.

Dear Hector,

You deserve answers, and I need to be free of this terrible secret I've held on to for so long.

I read Joan's letter in its entirety, and when I was finished, I refolded it, tucked it in the envelope, and shoved it into my pocket. I rested my hand on Frank's head and stared out over the valley.

I had been grappling with the what-ifs for years. I had

worked out my frustration and anger that had been growing in the last months with every hard swing of the hammer. And now that I had answers, I was not certain what I felt. It did not feel like relief or guilt or fury or helplessness, but some sweetly poisonous cocktail of every emotion I had struggled with from the moment the very man who played a role in taking my girls from me showed up on my doorstep to tell me they were gone.

I cleared my throat and dug my thumb and forefinger into my eyes to ease the burning sensation.

I wondered if Grover had noted the date. Today marked sixteen years since my girls had disappeared.

Grief was a strange creature. I had known all along my girls were dead. I had known the only way they would be returned to me would be in a casket or an urn. But there was a finality I had been robbed of for the last sixteen years that now stole my breath.

The ache beneath my ribcage felt so real I pressed a hand to my chest and wondered idly if I were having a heart attack. I thought after all these years, knowing would bring relief. It did, but it was accompanied by anger at the senselessness of their deaths and a new kind of grief that felt like a raw, exposed wound.

This new grief felt like the blistered, scorched expanse of earth the inferno in August had left in its wake.

The fire department had managed to save most of the homes on the western side of Raven's Gap, but the businesses downtown and the eastern side of town had been ravaged by fire. Only the inn, one street downtown, and one neighborhood had remained largely untouched by the fire.

It was a devastating blow. No lives had been lost,

though, and I knew firsthand how stubborn the people of Raven's Gap were. The town looked like a camper lot now as people worked to rebuild. Already a number of buildings had been resurrected.

William had stayed and taken up the commander's position at the police department as the previous commander took on the chief's position. When not working his shift at the station, he had loaned himself out to the construction crews in town to help with rebuilding.

Annie had undergone neuro-rehabilitation after recovering from the initial surgery. It took six weeks for the swelling and pressure in her brain to go down enough for the neurosurgeon to replace the bone flaps she had removed from Annie's skull. She had headaches regularly. Her vision blurred at times, and she became exhausted easily. When she grew tired, her ability to concentrate flatlined and she became confused and frustrated.

I had talked it over with her and the neurosurgeon, and we decided she would start high school in Gardiner next fall. Right now, she did distance learning courses at a slower pace so as not to overtax her still-healing brain.

She had spent most of her time home with Betty until the woman lost her battle with cancer last month. Ed and Jack's grief seemed to be mingled with relief that her long, painful struggle was over. Annie had taken her sharp decline and death the hardest.

I knew she had been frightened of Frank in the beginning, so it surprised me how much comfort the poodle offered her now. Most days, I lost my dog to the girl. He stuck close to her and abandoned me each night to sleep at her side. From the day she had come home, he had attached himself to her. Now when she became confused or frustrated, he soothed her as nothing else could.

I had asked her not to come with me to the build site this week. She divided her days between helping Ed at his newly rebuilt shop and helping Maggie and Evelyn at the inn.

When Faye Anders had transferred the inn's ownership to me, I had been at a loss. I didn't know what to do with an inn. Handing it over to Maggie after the diner was destroyed in the fire was the best use of it.

Ed and Maggie both insisted on paying Annie for the work she did, though they kept the tasks for her light and easy as she recovered. Already, she was talking about saving money for school. I did not tell her she didn't need to work and save money for college. When the time came, I would let her know about the fund I had created for her with the fifty thousand dollars I had set aside as a reward for information about Winona and Emma.

My eyes burned, and when I felt dampness on my cheeks, I did not bother to wipe it away. The wind would do that for me. I sat with Frank and my grief in the autumn sun as the afternoon edged into evening.

When I heard the rumble of an approaching engine, I knew who it was. Somehow Ed's ancient Chevy had survived the fire, and he had given it to Annie, though she was not allowed to drive by herself yet while she was still recovering.

Frank abandoned me and raced to the girl as she clambered out of the truck. Ed lifted a hand to me as he dropped her off and then turned his truck back toward town.

Her face was wreathed in smiles as she knelt and hugged the poodle. He leaned against her, his own canine smile on full display.

"How were your classes today?" I asked as she approached.

"I was able to study for two hours," she said proudly. "I was thinking that maybe when I start school next fall, I could try out for the track team."

"We can talk to your neurosurgeon. I think by then, that should be fine."

"I'll have track meets regularly." She said it with a careful casualness and kept her gaze on Frank.

"I'll be there," I said. "For each one. Ed and Maggie will want to come, too."

Family was a hard concept for both of us to grasp, it seemed, but we were trying.

"I have something to show you," I said.

She followed me inside the unfinished cabin, Frank trotting at our heels. The ceiling and walls were up, but the interior was still raw, the electrical and plumbing work exposed along the walls.

She stopped in the bedroom doorway with a gasp, eyes wide as she stared at the ceiling.

This was the reason I had asked her to stay away from the site this week. I shifted and cleared my throat.

In the aftermath of what had happened to her, she had become afraid of the dark and had frequent nightmares about being in that small room in Joan's basement with no light.

The skylight in the ceiling was the biggest one I had been able to find. I wondered if I had done the wrong thing when her eyes brimmed with tears. Before I could react, she walked into me, face pressed against my chest, arms tight around me.

I patted her shoulder awkwardly. A sob slipped free from her and shook her small frame.

"What's this about, kid?" I asked.

"You did this for me."

"I thought you might like to see the stars at night," I said. "I thought that might help."

She leaned back far enough to look up at me. Tears streaked down her face, and her lips trembled. "I wish you really were my dad," she whispered.

My throat closed. This time when she leaned into me, I did not hesitate to wrap my arms around her. I pressed my lips to the top of her head. For an instant, when I breathed in, I thought I caught the scent of strawberries, a scent I suddenly, vividly remembered always clinging to Emma's hair. I breathed in again, and it was gone.

"Any man," I said softly, "would be proud to have you as a daughter."

We stood like that for a long moment, Frank leaning against our legs. When she finally stepped back, she took a shaky breath and palmed away the dampness from her face.

"Are you still working on the roof?" she asked.

I nodded and moved back out to the porch. "Another day or two, and it'll be done. Then I can start on the inside."

"Can I help?"

I studied her in the evening light. She was changing. Tension and uncertainty no longer clung to her. She stood as tall as her short stature allowed, and she spoke plainly. She smiled and laughed more easily, though occasionally I caught her staring into the distance with the lines of her face tight with sadness and memory. Her hair was growing back.

I thought if Emma were still with me, the two girls would have been friends, and I hoped Winona would be proud of my belated efforts at fatherhood.

"We have an hour of daylight left," I said.

"And an hour before Maggie expects us over for dinner," she reminded me. "Ed and Jack are coming tonight, too."

"Then let's get busy."

Frank settled in a patch of sunlight on the porch with a sigh. I held the ladder as Annie climbed to the roof.

I paused with a foot on the rung and looked up to the ridge above the cabin. The slant of light over the mountains cast the ridge Winona had picked for a house in a golden gleam. I had built a bench up there, overlooking the view.

Some mornings, before the sun had risen and when the world was still and quiet, I hiked up there and sat on the bench. It was a good spot to watch the day break over the mountains. Every time I trekked up there, a blur of white kept pace with Frank and me through the trees. She always stayed just out of sight. Had Frank not sensed her presence as well, I would have thought I imagined her.

I climbed the ladder, and Annie and I worked side by side until the last light of day faded. She and Frank piled into my new truck as I put away my tools. I crossed the meadow that had already regrown through the ash but paused when I reached my truck.

I glanced again at the ridge above the meadow. The moon was rising over the mountains, and from the ridge came a wolf's haunting song welcoming the night's dawn.

Acknowledgements

This series would not exist if Jason Pinter had not taken a chance on me in 2018 when I queried him about a World War II story I had written. I owe him tremendous thanks for seeing potential in my writing.

Many thanks to the friends and family who have supported me in this journey, who have cheered for me, who have bolstered me, and who have come to each new story with enthusiasm and trust.

Special thanks to Michael, for a million reasons big and small. And, as always, endless gratitude to Aidan, who is game for anything as long as he's at my side.

About the Author

Meghan Holloway found her first Nancy Drew mystery in a sun-dappled attic at the age of eight and subsequently fell in love with the grip and tautness of a well-told mystery. She flew an airplane before she learned how to drive a car, did her undergrad work in Creative Writing in the sweltering south, and finished a Masters of Library and Information Science in the blustery north. She spent a summer and fall in Maine picking peaches and apples, traveled the world for a few years, and did a stint fighting crime in the records section of a police department. She now lives in the foothills of the Appalachians with her standard poodle and spends her days as a scientist with the requisite glasses but minus the lab coat.

She is the author of HIDING PLACE, HUNTING GROUND, KILLING FIELD, and ONCE MORE UNTO THE BREACH, all available from Polis Books.

Follow her at @AMeghanHolloway.

CPSIA information can be obtained
at www.ICGtesting.com
Printed in the USA
JSHW020831170622
27148JS00001B/1

9 781951 709860